Southword *44*

Southword is published
by Southword Editions
an imprint of the
Munster Literature Centre
Frank O'Connor House
84 Douglas Street
Cork City T12 X802
Ireland

Issue 44
ISBN 978-1-915573-02-5

www.munsterlit.ie

@MunLitCentre

/southwordjournal

/munsterliteraturecentre

#Southword

Editor
Patrick Cotter

Seán Ó Faoláin International Short Story Competition Judge
Alan McMonagle

Gregory O'Donoghue International Poetry Competition Judge
Suji Kwock Kim

2023 Subscribers' Competitions Judge
James O'Leary

Production
James O'Leary

Thank you to Anne Kennedy for her technical assistance

Cover Image: *'Hidden Fish'* (detail) by Anne Kennedy

The Munster Literature Centre is a grateful recipient of funding from

CONTENTS

Please Subscribe

By subscribing, you will receive new issues of *Southword* straight from the printers, as quickly as we will ourselves. Your subscription will also help to provide us with the resources to make *Southword* even better.

Rates for two issues per year:

Ireland, UK, North America, Australia, New Zealand	€20 *postage free*
Rest of Europe	€24 *postage free, tax-inclusive*
Rest of the World	€30 *postage included*

For subscriptions and renewals visit munsterlit.ie.

Southword may also be purchased issue-by-issue through Amazon outlets worldwide and select independent booksellers.

Two Poems
Abigail Parry

Some remarks on the General Theory of Relativity

Space, it turns out, curves.
                        Space itself.
        And time does too, or rather
space and time together curve and stretch
wherever there is matter. And this has always been the case,

but no one thought to tell me. Practically, this means
that if I lived up a mountain,
and my twin lived by the sea, then one or other of us
        would be younger than the other.

        I don't have a twin. I've got an older brother
who says we never landed on the moon.
An uncle, who thinks aliens are farming us as food,
who says The End Is Coming
                        and Coming Very Soon.
An aunt who liked cocaine – who had the Seven Sisters
tattooed across her back when she got clean.
And a father, who took off like a comet when he could,
who won't be coming back this way again,
not in this life.

                        As for me,
        my sense of things in general
is loosely sentimental. And outer space, with all its baudequin
        of quark and antiquark and light and dark
is no exception. I like the bits that look like us, that look
like human things.

A little spooky action.
Some unexpected pairing, locked in formal equilibrium.
I like the null and void of a black hole, but only
– let's be honest – as a vehicle
where the tenor is depression.
Beyond that, I find I'm fairly chilled
by distances and zeros, by emptiness and lack,
by the eerie little whine in the word *vacuum.*

Last night, washing dishes, I looked up to see my neighbour
staring at her sink, with all her dishes
piled beside her –
a mirror-trick, configured
by the way the houses here have of bending round each other.

Our paths don't ever cross – we keep our different hours –
but the houses here are small, the walls are thin.
I hear her talking, sometimes, on the phone,
I hear her cough at night. I hear the little *clunk*
of the cabinet in her bathroom –

the same cheap bathroom cabinet
that I have in my bathroom –
the same cheap clunking cabinet all landlords put in flats.
And yes, I must assume

she hears that little *clunk.* She hears me cough at night.
She hears me talking, sometimes, on the phone,
she's thought *These walls are thin.*
She's looked up from her sink to see her twin
in a square of yellow kitchen-light, with ten dark feet between.

– then the knife-edge found my finger, and it came up
red and sudden –
that scandalous reminder
of all that ties us down and ropes us off from one another.

Whatever happened to Rosemarie?

Your song is on the radio again, Rosemarie.
The one where every other line is *Rosemarie, Rosemarie.*
He acts likes he can't hear it, but I see it, Rosemarie –
how the backrooms of his brain have all lit up with ROSEMARIE.
A ten-foot neon sign, and it's flashing ROSEMARIE
in ten-foot neon letters, that go *Rose* and *mar* and *ee.*
And he's turning drunken circles arm-in-arm with Rosemarie
in a seedy little dive-bar. And the bar's called *Rosemarie's.*

I found a load of photographs – they're all of Rosemarie –
he keeps them in an album labelled *Me and Rosemarie.*
There's a little punctured heart above the R of Rosemarie
and it lives beneath the bed you chose together, Rosemarie,
the bed he shares with me. And he mumbles *Rssermuree*
when he's asleep and dreaming all his dreams of Rosemarie.
And I can't quite shake the feeling I'm intruding, Rosemarie,
when the springs inside the mattress squeal *Ro-semarie, Ro-semarie* –

Ro-semarie, Ro-semarie – Ro-semarie, Ro-semarie –

There's a signpost in his heart that points the way to Rosemarie
and beside it there's a suitcase that belonged to Rosemarie
and inside it there's a pocketbook inscribed with ROSEMARIE
with two tickets for the steamer ship, the *SS Rosemarie.*
Yes, the past's a foreign country, and its queen is Rosemarie,
and he worships at the altar of its Venus, Rosemarie.
I can't understand the language – every word is *Rosemarie*
and the picture in my passport couldn't pass for Rosemarie.

Someone sack the archer – he's *obsessed* with Rosemarie
and every dart is loaded with that poison, Rosemarie.
In every corner of my heart, there's a knife for Rosemarie
and they've all got secret nicknames – but the nickname's Rosemarie.
And in this light – and if I squint – he looks a bit like Rosemarie.
Just add a bit of lipstick... yes, like that, like Rosemarie.
Now tell me that you love me. Say your name is Rosemarie
and kiss me like she kisses. Say I'm yours, my Rosemarie.

1st Prize, Gregory O'Donoghue International Poetry Competition

When Our Mother Dies

Jenny Mitchell

after Sharon Olds

The nurse is over by the door, a parakeet
on the window ledge, sounds of a busy ward
close by. Our mother takes her final breath –
silence I have never heard before – no bird, no ward.
The nurse's mouth is moving as the door creaks
shut. Mother's lips begin to part, produce a field
of orchids on her tongue, the three-roomed shack
where she was raised. Her siblings playing in a field
are not grey-haired, back-bent or dead but running
wild – eight children dressed in rags including her
dancing near an oak, sticking out her tongue
to a bent-backed woman kneeling at a stream,
beating clothes on smooth, grey rock. Grandmother
reaches for the oak, yanks down a branch, thicker
than grandfather's arm – he's run away by now,
drunk no doubt with his rank women. Grandmother
rips leaves off the branch, attacks my mother's skin
till welts are what she strokes to help her fall asleep,
pain assigned my brother in due course. The parakeet
flies high above my mother's tongue. She walks
through all her ages – young woman with a child –
it was meant to be a moment's fun with a stranger
at a party on a bed of coats. She is caught again,
drags two children close behind, the field replaced
by concrete slabs, a high-rise flat. The branch becomes
a belt she hands to a strange man, not a father but
we're told to call him dad. He attacks her son. My brother

hides the welts – all this is on her tongue with the night
he took his final breath. The field returns with him –
back straight, head high – still twenty years of age.
She runs towards him as the bird flies off, and being just
the same as when he breathed, my brother does not turn away.

2nd Prize, Gregory O'Donoghue International Poetry Competition

Burying Grandfather

Yesol Kim

was what we did not do.
His body flown across the sea, pristine,

five pounds of ash. I remember
clouds parting where the plane wing
cleft: a scalpel drawn through water.
Father, dry-eyed beside me—

Liar.
I was not there.

My father flew alone.

A wind like cool silk through bluegreen willows. I remember this clearly but the willows were pines.

The firstborn took him to the mountains in the south. Plaques hammered in the terraced slopes. Jade staircase graved with names of the dead. The firstborn took him to a beautiful place. Grandfather did not ask for beauty; he asked to be scattered in his hometown. Gohyang. Or was it to end there? Either way. In memory, the dead have no say. The son is alive. The choice is his.

He asked to be scattered in his gohyang.

Northward, a village hemmed by hornbeam razed by a war.

What he yearned for most was not the house that raised him, but the mountains just beyond—

He would evade boy games to roam for hours, shell chestnut spikes with his bare palms.

Unlike other children, he knew to wait.

Paddy to forest. Daybreak to dusk.

Grinding nutmeat between molars, cold and scarcely sweet.

He watched time.

Time watched back.

Between them fleshed a bond for cutting, umbilical.

Once, a Siberian chipmunk scuttled down the bark imprinting itself into his spine.

Once, an alpine swift jabbed a jumping spider from rootfrost, the perch for his crossed feet.

Snow on his brow. His threadbare sleeves.

Patience so imperturbable, it outlasts the vigil of animals.

Shapeshifter, the child you were is not lost. He wants to play.

He hides-and-seeks the masquerades of your truest face.

For fourteen months in the nursing home, grandfather waited to die.

Grandfather did not ask for beauty.
We give him these things
for those who love the dead are selfish,
those who impose their will on that which has none—

His firstborn took the urn.
If the younger son had opposed to this—
My father came second; he has no say.
Uncle interred it in the south.

The mask he lies to—put it on.

Never

Judith H. Montgomery

after a photograph
Mariupol, Ukraine, 1941

She bends above the child clutched at her waist,
as though she could fold him back into her womb.

Her shot body hangs at the brink. Still, she hoists
the other, kneeling boy by one staunch hand,

as if to haul him back out of his future.
His naked feet slip at the forest rim of a ravine

choked with bodies whose present time is past—
history. But not, never, past. Today I hold

my grandson's hand high to keep him from a fall,
as he learns to shift up from his knees,

struggles to walk alone. I want to reach
into the cold photograph, seize the slipping child's

arm, lift him out of the shot into a different
present. But the frail print fixes him for death.

When this mother falls, all three will fall,
burdened by her dead weight. I cannot turn

away from the page burned on my sight,
or from a family that could be my own.

Can't erase her smoke-shrouded face:
stubborn mother who lifts the boy's body close

with her dying hand. Who says—without saying—
I've got you. I will never let you go.

Alphabet for a New Life

Nathalie Abi-Ezzi

she crosses the border
with a typewriter in her arms
and a baby in her belly

and in her mind a promise
that this typewriter shall never
again print German words

that this baby shall never
sculpt its thoughts
in the language that disowned
its mother;

that even now is hunting her
uniformed hounds hot on her heels
as she hauls the three of them
from one world to another

then waits for the signal
that will mean
carry on.

and as she waits
she disassembles all the words
she ever knew
and sends the particles
drifting letter by letter
through her veins

swirling downwards
until they find
the place where
her baby lies safely
curled;

directs them to sift
through the placenta and
– guided by the thrum of her heart –
to gather and hang
suspended

in other-worldly
unhatched dreams

an alphabet for a new life.

The Stones of Childhood Are Hard to Chew

Kizziah Burton

Husband forfeits our child to cover his debts.
No one says a word when my five-year-old
stumbles
under the tombstones bound to her
body in the granite quarry. She hauls
stacks for miles down into a sinkhole
and back, tonguing grit in her teeth
until her gums bleed and she coughs
up lost sounds tangled in a little red
string like the one her father's father
tied around her finger to remind her
she should always be nice.
She doesn't plot escape across the river
like some siddha travels without a boat.
She's not afraid of getting wet to pay
father's debt. Her grandmother's last
words, before she left her in the road,
were swift lessons in transmutation.
It's how water turns to ice
& ice turns to snow & snow turns to rain
& rain makes the flowers & quenches the cow's
thirst to make the milk you drink. Daughter
knows grandmother is only comforting
herself when she runs down a dirt road
to her son turning his back on his own.
My child knows dying has nothing to do
with milk as the woolly smoke creeps over
the water, like her breath pillows the cold.
She imagines herself washed
and combed, quiet as cloth, wrapped
and cast on the Ganges. Firelit, like I was –
chin tucked with prayers and incense, full
of sleep a girl can never sleep while living.
In her dream, she doesn't sink into mud
or silken skies with silvery ash. She dreams
the currents carry her to me, gently down
the stream, so we can wake up in another
country, where, like red and gold fruit,
stones grow softly.

For my younger children: a reminder of the far-flung diversity of your identities in the language of geography and theoretical physics

Simon Peter Eggertsen

Unasked, but so you will know, here is a recounting of
the quantum influences, the little arcs of familiar experience
that spark-form your identities:

(i) *charm:* the brown-girl songs of your West Indian *mother,*
the laced cosmology of questions in Caribbean folklore
—which village slave auntie first added a *deepa-greena*

taste, *chado beny,* to spice up the sloppy *callaloo?* How,
as giggling children, you learned to call the sharp reach
of the *sword plant—"mother-in-law's tongue!"*;

(ii) *strange:* encircling warps, the relativity embedded in
your *father's* quirky English thoughts—the size, the shape,
the spontaneity of a solar wind, now just a mild spring breeze

in Cambridge, as it twirls medallions of beveled clear glass
near Rose Crescent, the Sun, as it perfects its own prism work,
scatters soft spectrals, rainbows here and there;

(iii) *down:* the diminishing distance, the slowing rhythm
of Time your California *grandmother* intends to keep on either
side of the present, the spontaneous entanglement awaiting

the monarchs at Monterey Bay as they strand together at dusk,
camouflage in the eucalyptus, rest, tremble subtly, wait for
the blaze of morning's Sun to remind them they can fly again;

(iv) *up:* the pulsing quasars, the light-ladened flash of fireworks
set off by your Chinese *forefathers*—how they ricocheted red
off their dragon-arched village gate, split, curled, then scrawled,

like a child's quixotic sparkler writing, the strokes of ancient
calligraphy for *joy* and *luck* and *prosperity* in the New Year's
night air;

(v) *top:* your half-Danish *grandfather's* Wildwood, where
each morning the Sun has to fight for space in the narrow
canyon, the swinging bridge near quiet Dr. Weight's, where

each crossing was an adventurous leap, a rising toward some
kind of nervy blue limbo, whenever another child flexed
the bridge works back, lofting you up, away, standing you on air;

(vi) *bottom:* the expanding, smooth Space occupied by your island
grandmother's own black matter—as dense and lyrical as this
poetry—the event horizon of five female figures, draped as night

in their wind-blown *bui buis,* whorling along the cobblestones
of Gizenga Street, Zanzibar, the amount of light they swallow up,
then reflect back, as they slide their shade across a mosque's

sun-perfected presence, their words of peace, *"as-Salaamu-Alaikum."*

To The Muse of Zeros

Blair Ewing

Muse, accept this orphan howl
from one who won't
add to the family tree.

Guang gun, the Chinese would call me:
bare branch. I prowl
the empire's beaches,

even unto its farthest reaches
in search of my prey:
fossilized but still living

bits of languages & after cleaning
& chewing them longer than
Demosthenes, my mouth

gives birth to my golem-children, all
endowed with fractured speech
& flippered feet:

free to swim like a song in the Sea of Babel.

Cries of the Loon

Galin Elias Franklin

There came a day more bruised than burning in late September

When the air seemed to just snap, and a northerly chill closed in

On the lakes of Maine. Leaves of birch, beech and maple had begun

To fill with the flush of falling; sunlight filtering through

Would no longer cast jade on the water. That watershed morning,

Sweet must of lakewater rose up to grey bluster, scraps of grieving

Swirling about. We heard the common loon duetting far away

That near is too far in lake time—haunting whoops and wails tripartite.

Music of the changing season. Soon, the female would be heading

South without her mate. Down steps laced with browning pine needles,

We made for shore. You were all bundled up though still wearing shorts,

And I braced your slender shoulders above their cancerous pit.

By then, the loons were so much closer, diving down to feed

On fish that dwell among weeds. Graze and restore. Yearn for

Spring's return when the loons will lilt for the hazy shore beyond.

***

From the lake flows Messalonskee Stream through the towns of Oakland
And Waterville where it empties into the Kennebec River.
Just upriver, an abandoned pulp and paper mill looms,
Its downwind, sulfurous rot and yellowing foam gone for good.
(How we 'Black Syrians' and 'Canucks' fought each other for purchase).
There I've seen a lone loon madly flap its wings, thrust out its great neck
And slowly, barely lift to stilted flight, passing right under
The Winslow bridge and down the Kennebec: downeast to where
Crystal blue ice was harvested and shipped as far as Calcutta;
Downeast to the island off Richmond where the Kennebec chieftain
Held forth from his palace fort; downeast past Merrymeeting Bay where
English colonists appeared out of the weltering, white-capped cold.
Early December, temperatures plunged and the lake froze over.
Without enough open water to take off, the loon was trapped,
Crashing into ice over and over as he tried to gain flight.

***

The loon becomes a dark field dappled with the first snowfall,

This neck of the woods glazed up to the sun-eye nearly breaking through.

Withered and tangled, vast earth endings that overlap the cove

Clutch all day long at air and snow. Here and there, pines are set adrift.

Now the woodland mist creeps ghostly down: out of nowhere, the moon.

I can hear my own echo cracking and breaking against the shore…

I'm lost in this world without you—In this world so very lost

Without you—Without you I'm lost

Small Towns

Peggie Gallagher

In Ireland a man must have a home town,
somewhere to leave behind him...
—Kerry Hardie

All things come to an end:
Summer dresses in shop windows,
Friesian cattle in the new grass,
the yellow flare of whins,
roadside Marian Shrines.
Do all things come to an end?
No. They go on forever.

Fitful sunshine under a threatening sky,
a sheugh of crushed ice under the wheels,
the mottled bark of un-leafed trees,
that gaunt flat-roofed house being obscured
by sycamore, birch and willow saplings.
Do all things come to an end?
No. They go on forever.

The church on the hill in the shelter of evergreens,
the bells, the chant, the murmur, a whiff of incense,
the dark-eyed grandchildren.
And the talk, the talk goes on forever.
The funeral procession around the long curve of the village,
the family back from London, Chicago, Perth.
These patchwork fields they know by heart.
These are the salt-sting days of remembering,
a part of them broken and faltering,
walking, as they walk now
past fields bright with new lambs, new grass,
past the limestone steeple,
up the incline to the brow of the hill.

This would always be the place
where they gather
for the lifting, steadying,
and shouldering the long box into the cuff of the wind,
taking the last weight of their father,
through the open gates
and lowering him into the clay of his forebears.

Cillní

Peggie Gallagher

It was a long journey for the man's pain.
No road let him see its path ahead.
The death of a son
can be told only to a stone.

No road let him see its path ahead
and nobody said a thing.
The death of a son can be told
only to a straggle of whitethorn,

and nobody said a thing.
His lonely ritual on a winter night;
only a straggle of whitethorn,
in a burial place cold and ancient.

His lonely ritual on a winter night;
birth's dark blade of grief
in a burial place, cold and ancient.
That mother-ache beyond bearing,

birth's dark blade of grief;
their unnamed, his small change of breath.
That mother-ache beyond bearing
that followed all their years.

Their unnamed, his small change of breath,
his pale cold limbs
that followed all their years.
Then tears turn to stone.

Then tears turn to stone.
The death of a son
that followed all their years
can be told only to a stone.

Extinction

Luisa A. Igloria

In stockyards, a Judas goat will lead
 sheep to slaughter, while its own life
is spared; with scent
 of estrus, will lure
 other goats out from behind rock and scrub
 so a helicopter rifle shot
can pick them out, one by one
 by one—*A little world*
within itself, wrote Darwin:
 with pools where blue-
 footed boobies come to wade, and
 tortoises old as boulders. Once,
a neighbor told me of the family dog
 they had to give away
when they moved;
 how her new owners said
 she limped back to the house they used to own,
 and lay down under the laurel tree
to die. What do the leaves say
 when they move like mouths
as the light changes, as little buds of jasmine
 continue to give up scent
 even as a different color takes over
 their pale ghost bodies?
All our dead come back to us
 in dreams so we can make apology.
They hold out sheets of our tears,
 so much silver warming
 the grass neatly clipped where we lie down
 to live out the rest of our days.

On the Night of Your Deployment

Gary V. Powell

I stayed up later than I should
turning the world over like
a melon in my hands

searching mountains and valleys
for places that didn't bristle
with broken bones

listening for oceans and lakes
with sweetly rolling waves
to sing a sailor home

then last minute I called you to say
stay safe and watch your six
stuff us dads say to sons

and you replied there's no glory
in staying safe and later you
posted that rockface pic

the one where you free-soloed
Linville Gorge and claimed
it gave you great peace

like the greatest peace you'd
ever known and I guess
that's when I knew

there are no places on this earth
without teeth and no gentle
seas without storms

and if you weren't in a desert
surrounded by people who
wanted to kill you

you'd be hanging off a mountain
secured only by your fingertips
searching for a foothold.

The Washpoosh Man

Greg Rappleye

1967

He'd come tumbling down Randolph Street
crying "Washpoosh! Washpoosh!"
those days he'd slip free and fast-walk
past Mam's sorry rental—his mouth a-grimace,
a wool cap pulled low over his musk-melon head,
galoshes, flannel shirt buttoned at his throat
and loose tail flying, eyes darting past our
garden and down the block toward Canal Street
and the herring sheds beyond.
We'd make little screams and swoon behind parked cars
and when his ancient father came trotting down
the hill, shouting "Where's Declan?
Where's he gone?" we'd pop up and point
toward Stoddard Lane, angling away two blocks
north, where the Washpoosh Man might be
at the Rexall scrounging for penny candies,
or worse, at the tavern across the way,
his hand waggling at his *dada* mouth,
mummering for a beer. If Anne Costello was working
at Rexall, she'd give Declan some Bit O' Honeys
or a few pieces of butterscotch, wrapped
in crinkly yellow cellophanes, before walking him
to the door. But if he went for the tavern
there'd be a broken Rock-Ola, and those no-account
longliners, with codfish knives hidden in the cabs
of their battered pickups, ready to torment Declan
in any ways Dexedrine and sloe gin might impel,
unless Perfect Ed was wiping the bar that day
in his bow tie, his white apron and starched shirt,
as he'd once seen bar-men dressed at an oyster house
in Boston. Near the taps he'd lay a 34-inch Louisville Slugger,
pull Declan a short draft, scrape the foam and go on
about the Red Sox or the scuttlebutt from Pleiku
(our town had Marines there—dug in, thumping mortars),

as Declan stood at the bar, mewling "Washpoosh,"
but quietly, in those few moments after
he'd found refuge; all before his ancient father pulled open
the ding-a-bell door, mumbled a hard oath,
and tugged at Declan's cuff to lead him home.

Photo Essay

Photographs by John Minihan of Havana, Cuba

Alicia Alonso (1920 – 2019) who helped to transform her native Cuba into a world centre for classical ballet. Photographed in her ballet school in Havana, 2011.

John Minihan pictured in Havana, 2011. Photographed by Deirdre Callaghan.

Sculptor José Ramón Villa Soberón pictured with his life-size bronze statue of writer Ernest Hemingway at El Floridita Bar, Havana, 2019.

Former Cuban Ambassador to Ireland, Noel Carillo pictured at the memorial for the Hunger Strikers at Victor Hugo Park, Vedado, Havana, 2018.

Music is everywhere in Havana. 2018.

Everything is repairable. Cobbler, Havana, 2011.

Havana, 2018.

Newspaper seller, Havana, 2018.

Havana, 2020.

Workers relax, Havana, 2018.

Cuban workers, Havana, 2018.

Classic American cars for the tourists, bicycles for the locals, Havana, 2010.

Two Poems
Aidan Mathews

Marlboro Man

You were there at my side when I lost my virginity.
You were there, joined at the hip, when I found it again.

Through the years of night-terrors on memory foam,
Of change for the payphone in the closed ward,

And in the basilica on the lake among the barefoot
And the monastery on Mount Athos for the Easter Vigil;

Along the yellow-brick road of the El Camino Real,
As a post-grad High Plains drifter in Palo Alto,

Writing poems about the peripheries from the centre of power
While the Mexican wetbacks rolled out lawn from a trailer truck;

In the Tenderloin streets with the X's and no Franciscan,
On the island paths to the temples one cigarette distant;

At the shape-shifts of her belly like a sand-dune, drifting;
At the Moses crib in the corner, at my AWOL stool-weaving;

With a daughter, the pee and nicotine of our walkabout,
Who would suck my cigarette finger like an inhaler

As I lay in a Lithium pool of the salt Dead Sea
Where the hills are levelled and the valleys are filled in;

And on 9/11, when I sat on the edge of my bed at the plasma set
With my unwashed feet in a moon of talcum powder.

Until today, after rainfall, the sky smiling through its tears,
Amidst a meteor shower of my own floaters,

I can see on the MRI a murmuration of shades
That have risen up, fuming, from the grey waste of my seashell ashtray

To leave me open-mouthed at last, to leave me breathless,
My worry-beads, my rosary, my jailer's clutch of house-keys,

My morning prayer, companion of the small hours,
Ashram of the angle-poise, of the wry pause and the line-break.

As smoke is driven away, Psalm something, so am I driven.
Now I do for you as you will do for me. I scatter your ashes.

Doors Opening, Doors Closing

I soar to the third floor of a hospital
In a mirrored lift like a three-leaf dressing table
To a glacier of white walls, white ceiling lights, white sheets,
The snow-glare of a ward like Newfoundland.

I am being prepped, old friend. You are for post-mortem.
A name-tag on my wrist, a name-tag on your toe.
They are close-shaving my pubis. You will be embalmed.
The same chaplain will bring us Extreme Unction,

Two lots of loved ones pay the same parking toll,
And the same soprano voice in the elevator
Will tell us all: Doors opening, doors closing.
A century back, when we were undergraduates,

Full of paradox and the pleasures of oxymoron,
We'd have pulled some pretty girl out of the Arts Block
In a gypsy skirt, drop earrings, and a pair of espadrilles
With our dialectical flirting.

A packet of ten Major cost thirteen new pence,
And Time Now Please called for a round of lager.
If the hip chick slid her tongue into your mouth,
You could tease her muslin breast with your cigarette finger.

Now, late by several years for my own funeral,
I'm waiting here in a gown for my wife's kidney
And the stitch-in-time of a smiling seamstress surgeon.
The only sense you'll find is in symmetry,

You'd say, *not in the sign of the question mark*
But the figure eight cut into meltwater
Like a double negative that dissolves zero.
I hold the morphine pump like a child's snow-globe

And the voice in the concrete shaft says: Doors opening,
Doors closing. Stand well back.
In a ward, one floor above my little ascension,
They are stripping your parts like a saint's relics.

There's a new cornea for a roofless temple
Of the Holy Ghost in Mullingar, maybe,
Another for a roadside shrine in Ballinasloe;
Heart, lungs, and a teetotaller's liver

By helicopter and motorbike courier
To those who are neither Jew nor Gentile,
Neither you nor me. They are sheathed in ice-packs
And not in amethyst or in ivory caskets

While the ransacked body in the lift going down,
Wrapped in white linen on a hostess trolley,
Unsettles the two young thirtysomethings
With my iphone charger and Dairy Milk chocolates

Who are waiting to rise from the basement floor
To a patient whose chest wears a port like a bull's eye.
He has taken off both of his black Bose earbuds
To hear those accordion curtains fold and unfold.

The Lady and the Storyteller
Paddy Bushe

for Seán Mac a' tSíthigh

It was in his bones before he was born,
The island mountain that had stretched

Itself lazily into the sea for centuries
Or reached mysteriously into clouds

In search of the old gossip and stories
That he, in turn, told to the islanders.

But when the lady, speaking *de très*
Haut en bas, and carefully marshalling

Every last weapon in her armoury
Of superiority, belittled the storyteller's

Mountain, along with all its imaginings
Through the generations, and explained

How valueless his old stories were
(even those told by the mountain)

How confused his languages were
(especially those she did not speak)

He drew her as a stick-doll, a cartoon
He carried from the base to the very

Summit of the mountain, where he let
The wind take it, then watched it drift

And diminish out of vision, accompanied
By the raucous mockery of seabirds.

Ar mh'anam, he whispered, *ach feasta*
Ní bheadsa ag sodar i ndiaidh na n-uasal.

Prisoner's Lament

Canisio Mudzimu

Malnourished prisoners packed like kapenta fish in the tiny cell
outrival me for sleeping space in the overcrowded gaol.
Thin, tattered blankets emitting an acrid, dungeon smell
barely protect my frail, anorexic body from imminent freezing.

Overfed lice reproducing in the bosom of the blankets
spring to action at the hint of my falling asleep,
draining my blood until it almost runs dry
as I fidget agonisingly in unison with the sound of my faint cry.

Bruised face, swollen feet – a fine product of torture,
inflicted for minor transgressions by the baton sticks of the prison guards.
I am physically weak, mentally-drained & spiritually annihilated,
thanks to shackles, kwashiorkor of freedom & physical deprivations.

At the sound of alarm bells, I spring into feeble action,
impatiently waiting for the jailors to open the huge metal doors,
to be greeted by fresh air & sunlight in the prison yard –
a major relief after spending 14 hours without seeing light.

I struggle to swallow the nutrient-poor prison gruel,
sitting on the bare, torturous ground with a vengeance of its own,
my torn gaol garb making a scarecrow of me,
I pray to tear myself free from the shackles of captivity.

Metamorphosis

Karan Kapoor

"I believe in mirrors."
—Alejandra Pizarnik

Last night I saw my father, he had the eyes of a gandharva. I do not say this ambulanced by sentiment or in false hope or to unveil I knew before last night how the eyes of a gandharva could or could not look. He wasn't half-horse and half-bird leaping on the black keys of the invisible piano of the wind. Nor did I hear his celestial voice, muted singer at the height of his stupor. His body as if he'd been redeemed from flames and his eyes either the eyes of a gandharva or not quite belonging to his body anymore. Then he blinked. Camouflaged with sun, he meandered to the other side of the mirror and from the past erased the syntax of his sobbing. He said he wants to live forever, like a ring on a dead man's hand. This is his duty to whisky. Orion in the distance disembowels. Embracing god's shadow in a trance, his bones arch like grapevines. The night fumes blue, closes like an elegy. He has transmogrified into another species, and is no longer my father.

Infestato
E.M. Hughes

1st Prize, Seán Ó Faoláin International Short Story Competition

We communicate through the walls. They carry on a muffled conversation in Italian, I yell back in English. They stamp on their floors, I hit my ceiling with the butt of a sweeping brush. Doors are constantly slamming in the rooms below me, next door they play thumping techno music, or they fuck on an old springy bed. But mostly they just talk, loudly, all around me, in big Italian voices.

Today is particularly bad. Next door a woman is screaming at someone about something, a child, a man, a dog. Maybe her mom, over the phone. Above me they are moving their furniture, dragging it like thunder rolling across the floor. A tell-tale sign that soon they will pump up the volume of some bass-heavy music system, while they jump, or skip, or just stamp in place. Who knows?

I raise the volume of the television to the max. It is an old blockbuster of a TV that came with the apartment. You can only get a good view of it by sitting directly in front of it, from any other angle it is impossibly opaque. At its max volume it spits out a garbled melodrama in staticky Italian. There are no English channels.

I give up on reading and start doing some squats in the middle of the room.

I am starting to get pretty heavy around the waist.

Outside my window I see twenty different people walking the same dog every day. I'm only on the fifth floor so I have a pretty good view of the narrow pedestrian path that runs between the parking lot of the apartment block and the empty motorway. The same podgy cocker spaniel led on the same ratty pink lead, taking the same piss on the same yellowed patch of concrete. Just a different person every time. This is how I get to know my neighbours. I see in succession a young man in a muscle-T with a greased back coiffure, a teenager in fluffy pink pyjama bottoms, red lipstick and makeup, headphones too big for her head, I see a squat man in a full suit, wiping sweat from his bald head, a bell-shaped lady with a close crop of grey curls and a cooking apron, and I see other configurations of: kids, tired-looking parents and skinny, hungry-looking teen boys in tracksuits who might be intimidating in a group but by themselves just look kind of lonely. But always the same fucking dog, wagging its tail with endless enthusiasm. I try to pair the faces and bodies with the noises that permeate my apartment day and night but fail.

I've sussed out that they are all sharing the same dog to get themselves in a walk, and that I am the only gobshite not in on the racket.

On Friday nights, the murmurs to my left, my right and below me, rise and converge above me in the ceiling. Music thumps, glasses clink.

I would have liked to joke with my mam that it was like having an infestation of gigantic rats in the crawl space.

Twice a week my groceries are left in a brown box on the mat in front of my door. When the bell rings, if I am fast and lucky, I might catch a glimpse of the shoulder and rubber heel of the person who delivered it, as they follow their corpse down the stairs. I can never tell if it is a man or a woman.

In the first weeks of the shut-in, I got up at 7am every morning, shaved and put on a fresh shirt. I spent some time finding the best angle and background for the camera, but all the white walls looked yellow.

By now I have what you might call, charitably, a neck beard, and I tend to get up only when lying down becomes more tiresome than standing. Since what I would have described to my mam as my 'career setback' a few weeks ago, time has really stopped meaning all that much. Often I don't bother dragging myself the three metres from the couch to the open plan bedroom.

Most of the time I just stay on the couch all night. Really it's more like I am sitting on the couch and it's night and then, moments later, I am still on the couch but orange light is oozing in through the lace curtains in the corner of the kitchen.

I think I might be a ghost. The curtains do nothing to dissuade me. A spirit trapped in a Neapolitan apartment block, haunting its innocent denizens with bangings, the smell of unwashed hair and off milk, and a general sense of malignancy.

I really should learn the language, if only to make for a more informed spirit. Under a pile of junk mail and pizza boxes that I cannot fit into the narrow garbage chute in the hall, I recover the language books. I'd bought them for a course I was planning to attend in my first weeks in Naples, before they cancelled that and everything else.

Have you ever read Frankenstein? Well there is this bit, it's never in any of the movies, where the monster learns German by creeping in on this peasant family and stealing their copy of Milton. Puff, just like that, he's fluent. Not that it helps. The moment he speaks with them, they chase him off with torches and pitchforks, I think.

For me, a copy of Dante open, on its tenth page and resting on my knee, the babidy beeping of my neighbours never becomes anything other than noise. A noise that is loud enough to cut right through the full volume millennial rock pouring directly into my eardrums, but somehow never loud enough for me to make out distinct words.

But hey, the weeks go by, my beard gets long (though still only on the neck) and here we are, progress. I learn to say words like 'Immunocompromessi' when I order things by phone, repeating it slowly, again and again until I hear 'si'. I also learn the word 'solitudine', though I have no one around to correct my pronunciation.

It gets to the point where I can follow quarrels that start in the ceiling, bang through the room next door, and collapse into tears below me.

I have a dream of opening up my little kitchen window (it's bigger in the dream) onto a pastel-coloured day and lighting up a cigarette. It's all highly saturated colours, accompanied by a rustic guitar riff, like a goddamn pasta commercial. In the dream I call out to the dog walkers in fluent Italian, and they call back, and we chat, and they ask me 'oh my, how long have you been there?!' all shocked and inviting me for wine and carbonara and whatever. Don't get any ideas; it's the little old lady, not the girl in pyjama pants. And I call back to the old mare, I tell her that I'd love to but I can't, then I give her the whole sad spiel and she says, nodding sadly, 'oh my, oh my'. And then I realize she is speaking English and that this is a dream and I wake up.

Or I open my eyes. I get off the couch and try the kitchen window again. I pull the handle down and yank it hard towards me. Like every time I tried before, I can only open it about two inches. I can't tell if this is a mechanical flaw or a feature, some anti-suicide thing. I pretend to light up a cigarette and puff fake smoke out the narrow gap. The air outside, and this could be in my head mind you, smells like dog urine.

But really, I am just like Frankenstein. The monster I mean. Now when I stamp my foot on the floor loud enough I hear clear as day 'vaffanculo!' and I revel in being part of a 'vendetta'.

I decide to have a few beers. I don't normally drink alone, but out of nowhere there was a six pack in my grocery box. Two days later there was another, and then another. I called the grocery company, but they didn't get what I was complaining about. Neither did I really.

They were all room temperature of course; my fridge is very small. So when in Rome. Or Naples. I drink and drink and get to thinking about that ghost thing again. I think it's very funny, actually, to be a ghost in the flesh. I drink another warm beer. Before I know it I am racing around the room, banging on the doors, walls, ceiling, floor, kicking over my coffee table, breaking glasses, spewing fresh new romance curses from Irish lips.

I collapse on the floor and am surprised to find myself there. So surprised that I just start laughing, and don't stop until, at some point, I pass out on that spot of the dirty old carpet.

Now I am definitely asleep. I dream that I am at this crowded graveyard. There were like twenty or thirty funerals going on at once, and it's raining and also hot, and everyone is wearing a raincoat. It is that awful clammy way it gets on a busy bus on a wet day at home. I am at the graveyard and I am looking for my mam's grave, and I keep asking everyone I see, and they are all the dog walkers: the girl in pyjama bottoms but in a black suit, and the old lady with the thick curls in a black suit, and that little fellow in his black suit and the cocker spaniel too, still with its ratty pink leash. No one knows where my mam is, which makes sense, cause it's my dream and my party, and I don't know where she is.

There are hushed voices beneath me. Mind you, my ear has been pressed right against the floor this whole time. It's the sad little voices of a lady and a child. I start thinking, as I tend to do, about those voices, and wondering if it would make a difference if I could somehow match them all up with the right faces. Me knock, knock, knocking on the walls, and apologizing in simple, plain, but honest and well-meant Italian. Them delivering, not the old lady 'cause that's dangerous these days, but the others delivering a bottle of red wine, a peace offering, an overdue housewarming gift, and lingering in the hall, a few metres away, trying to talk, them in broken English, me in broken Italian. I start knock, knock knocking on the different gravestones, and somehow, it's only the English apologies coming out of my mouth that wake me up again.

For once I am in my bed, the sheets are all twisted and knotted around me like a rope.

I tie the rope tight around the pipe that runs along the ceiling of the kitchen. I give it a good yank to test it. The last thing I do is write the word 'Infestato' on the wall above that old TV, in the same paint I used to whiten the walls when I first moved in.

I knot the rope, wrap it tight. I am falling.

I have opened the kitchen window and am abseiling down the side of the building, down down down, past the windows of the rooms below, one, two, looking into the bright yellow rooms at the people in their natural habitats, the old lady cooking, the man in the muscle-T working out, the girl in pyjamas doing her lipstick, the dog, with a room of its own. Down, down, down. I am falling. The rope tightens.

Or I open my eyes.

Draíocht

J.P. Garvey

2nd Prize, Seán Ó Faoláin International Short Story Competition

The taxi driver didn't clock the big hare watching them through the ivied 'V' of the stile. "Grand quiet spot," he said, looking at the old schoolhouse before he drove off. And when his passenger looked again the hare was gone too. Strange to see one so near a dwelling. Maybe she had young leverets in the overgrown grounds.

The red front door and the windows with their little, red-muntined panes had a fairytale look. The deadlock lock turned clunkily, three hinges creaked. Motes swirled like tiny galaxies through evening sunbeams in the warmed-up fust. Opposing mirrors used to each other's emptiness regarded him from either end of the long hall.

It was mid-September. He was 'airing' the half-converted school for the owners, his sister and her husband, who were arriving in three weeks with their twin toddlers. There was little to be done apart from opening windows; removing dead bluebottles and cobwebs. All services were in place. Even the phone purred when he lifted it; and he suspected that they had invited him there for his own healing rather than to be of any help to them.

The first few mornings he sat in a suntrap with books, pens and paper; read, wrote and drank instant coffee; listened to the radio. He was sad; more like bereft. Sometimes he cried. Even the banalest pop songs could set him off. Occasionally he cried out when a particularly hurtful memory assailed him.

On one such tristful mid-morning he was visited by a man, a hurrying high-stepping man used to overstepping wet grass and rushes. In very long shorts, green wellingtons and a floppy beige hat, he looked more like a butterfly hunter who'd forgotten his net than a farmer. He shot past the half hidden table and doubling back spotted the new resident.

"You would be Jack?" he said, using the interrogative subjunctive of local quizzing.

"That'd be me," Jack answered in the same tense.

"You'd be Mary's brother?"

"I would – and you must be Walter."

"That's me, Wally," – offering his hand, reverting to simple present. "I brought you a few logs, the evenings can be chilly, I left them by the door; I live over the road if you're stuck for anything else at all, just give us a shout."

Then after asking the many questions his neighbourliness seemingly entitled him to, he queried finally, "And have you seen the hare yet?"

And when Jack said, "I have," Wally said "Hah! Kitty's back so."

An Indian summer which became the warmest and longest in living memory set in. But the lengthening nights were cold under clear skies. Nightimes he couldn't bear to be alone with his aloneness; so each evening he walked the two miles to the local village. He'd set the fire, shower while the dinner was cooking, eat and leave.

Mostly he went to a bar with the name 'GERS' above the door. Everybody, courtesy of Wally, knew who he was. Ger pronounced 'Jurr' by the locals was the owner. He had a gift for making one feel welcome: neither too warm nor too standoffish. Sometimes there'd be music.

"Maybe you'd give us a song Jack," he might say to be inclusive during open mike times. Jack made sure he never got that drunk – for a long time.

It was an old-fashioned two-classroom National School: untaught in for generations. At first he slept in a lower bunkbed in one of the little converted offices at the front but later moved his mattress into the 'Master's' classroom to catch the dawn light through the high windows. This was divided from the other, the 'Miss's' classroom where the little ones would have been taught, by a locked, full height partition.

Each night he lit the turf and log fire and read himself to sleep surrounded by its dancing shadows; dozed restless to the half-heard whisper of its settling embers; or woke abruptly to sea-winds rattling the big sashes. It was usually peaceful at night – quiet at any rate. A quiet sometimes so wound it almost ticked to confirm itself; but no sense of glower or eldritch. Nevertheless he always slept facing the fire.

Most afternoons he went for long walks by winding roads through wooded hills and whitethorn hedges; meandering in and out of seaview vantages; crossing streams over humpbacked stone bridges; watching oblivious otters or herons or just immersing himself in the pastoral rhythms everywhere around him: the updated rhythms of his childhood. By now all the local farmers (well done Wally!) knew who he was. They smiled and waved from cars and tractors.

For a while, on suntrap mornings, hidden behind the rampant, puce-berried alders and the fuchsia with its blossoms in blue mini-skirts he'd weep at a sentence from Neruda or Yeats that nailed his sadness. But slowly, with intermittent lapses he began to come to terms with the loss of Fiona. Sometimes he'd even get a Resurrection-feeling as of a heavy weight being rolled aside; of something unbearable overcome; fresh sunlight on his face and limbs.

He found an old, iron cart-axle to lift: every day an extra repetition or two till he managed fifty: redefining the muscles of first manhood: haymaking muscles, turf-cutting muscles, dormant muscles of memory. He grew fit and tanned playing hurl-squash in shorts against the back wall. Once when chasing a ball whose rebound he'd missed, he saw it roll beside the strangest little blue-grey carpet of down that floated an inch above the concrete yard as though borne up by magic. A thin smoky trickle joined the sidling carpet. Following this trickle back to its source he was mesmerised to see a hawk plucking a woodpigeon. It placed one talon on the half-butchered bird and tore off the breast-down with its curved beak. Golden-eyed, black pupiled, it swivelled its neck till its hooked and bloodied beak seemed aligned with its tail and observed him coolly. "This is triple augury," the fierce eyes said. "Go soothsay if you dare." Then it dragged the pigeon under a shrub and continued to pluck and gollop. A jess like a convict's iron was attached to its standing leg.

Draíocht lingered too on the little farms: in the middle of silage-shaven fields fairy bushes flourished undesecrated like leafy, haw-berried moles. The big hare driven from her ancient habitat recalled Kitty, the vengeful shape-shifting spirit.

The village was an old, long inhabited place. The ruins of a big monastery sacked by Cromwellian soldiers looked out on the estuary. At dusk its deep leyline peace seemed only heightened by the passing noise of engines and machinery. Its quiet harmony only enhanced after dark by the heavy splashes of fish jumping under the bridge or single seabird cries from saltwater.

In the pub he confined himself to three pints and a whiskey chaser, a small intake for him but enough to enhance the faery of the walk home. On those nights when he left the sea-sounds of the coast road and turned uphill towards the schoolhouse, stopping to listen to the sighs of dozing cows or the curt rips of their grazing; hearing a disturbed rooster complaining into general silence or, one time, patting a horse that nickered and leaned to him over a five-barred gate, he was back in the farmlands of his childhood.

Soon he knew every silhouette: the old wreathed beech with two outstretched arms longing for a hug; the rowan leaning slightly with one arm down like a pissing drunk; the big hairstyles of lone whitethorns and the tall stoic dryad in the stately scotch fir. The empathy of trees: how the hedgerow extroverts took the shape of animals or leaned out to greet you and sad that they couldn't, listened carefully and rustled their autumn foliage when you told them you understood their roots and rings; the smooth young skin inside their weather-beaten barks.

Once he sat on a dry stone wall to regard a late orange moon rising twig by twig through the stark, black arms of a dead ash.

Once in a trance, he watched from a height the silvery moon-ripple dazzle in the bay; an Underworld twilight veil the patchwork fields, until a dawdling cloud turned jewel edged again as the emerging moon pushed deeper gloom back under the bushy mearings. Wrapt, he watched till a terrible high register scream ripped his reverie. It came from behind a double-ditch directly above where he stood. An instant of terror eased almost immediately: it was no banshee, just a hotted vixen wailing her desire. He stayed motionless. She was very close. She hadn't sensed him else she wouldn't have shrieked. But though he hardly breathed for minutes, whether frightened or requited, she didn't cry out again.

His sister and family came and stayed a fortnight. He moved out into the ramshackle chalet at the bottom of the garden and slept in the top bunk. Every morning, early, the toddlers came to visit him. There was a hole in the bottom rail of the chalet door and he could see their little cherubic feet and calves in identical pairs of sandals; then he'd hear their erratic palm-knocks on the lower panel, and then,

"Nuncle Jack." Pause. Then, 'slap-slap' pause and again, "Nuncle Jack":

Always Paddy, the brown-eyed boy, making the action and the call; the little girl just standing back, watching. They didn't give up and eventually he climbed down and joined them. Other times he babysat while doing bits of DIY – repairing the chalet door or a window. Now he had company he read less and wrote only in his diary.

He soon got to know the little personalities. The boy, dextrous, gifted with shape-puzzles, a busybody liable to get into scrapes, a climber, a worry. The girl watchful, shy but knowing, making eye-contact, nodding in agreement when she understood. An older soul if you believed that sort of stuff.

"What you doin'?" she might ask taking her bottle from her mouth as a grandad might remove his pipe. Then having sucked a while to ruminate, she'd remove the bottle again and just to enjoy the new magic of repartee, ask the same question in her deep little baby-voice and repeat the answer to savour the sound.

Once when she seemed troubled and inclined to cry, he said, "Nonie are you ok – are you tired?" And she nodded vigorously as if at twenty months she knew exactly what might make her cranky.

"And would you like to lie down so?" And again the decisive nodding and she put her small plump hand out and they walked hand in hand to the room where her low bunk-bed was. He lifted her gently in and then sat and talked softly to her while her eyelashes wavered up and down until finally they covered her very blue pupils, then the blue-rinse eye whites and finally the bottle slipped from her lips and she slept.

"Where Nonie?" Paddy said flying through another big-pieced jigsaw.

"In bed Paddy, would you like to sleep too for a while?" He shook his head and galloped away towards the front door.

Another time when their parents were delayed and they'd grown restless and weepy he changed their nappies. No safety pins now and throwaways straight in the bin. But still no joke. A memory of younger siblings came back to him: nappy rash and baby-powder, Sudocreme and clean baby smell; testing warm milk on the tender inside of the forearm to get it perfect for baby mouths.

He read to them, perched one on each knee; perfect cherub fingers pointing crookedly at pictures; repeating the novel phrases. His arms around them a living safety rail locked at the baby book. The powerful rush of protective love vibrating through every fibre almost longing to be proved.

"I'm not going to live in some twelve storey council block in Benefitown. Broken lifts and a smell of piss," Fiona shouted. "That'd be some life alright: two mature students bringing up a child in a no-hope shithole!

Fifth floor of No Hope house. No, No! No way. Never!"

And then she sobbed for ages. There was no argument: She was right if she felt right. Her body. Righter than you could ever be no matter what you felt. And let's be honest: what did you feel? Pressure? A kind of macho guilt? And there would be plenty of time for children; later when things were... well, better.

And things *were* better when they'd got their degrees and found well paid jobs and a two-bedroomed flat. Only then she wasn't in love with him anymore. She met someone else and left him. He was shocked at the amount of pain a break-up that seemed so unremarkable when it happened to others could cause him.

After his sister and family returned to the city he found forgotten baby-books and toys lost throughout the unshorn grounds; a box of Cheerios in the cereal cupboard. He missed the children.

A change seemed to come over the atmosphere in the old school. Often in the evening dusk there were peripheral movements in the long hall; which always, when he turned quickly to check, transpired to be his own movements re-reflected in the opposing mirrors. His brother-in-law had told him that the sudden sepulchral moaning that began to sound occasionally from the far end of the corridor was due to a dodgy freezer in the partly converted younger schoolchildren's bathrooms. They'd checked it together and found that it happened sometimes when the thermostat kicked in or out.

Now that he was alone again its human groans sometimes woke him.

One evening a few days after the others left, when he'd gone there for frozen fish fingers, he'd used one of the nearby children's toilets. They were small and low with long chains to flush the high cisterns. While he washed his hands in a low washbasin the freezer did its moan-bellow.

Later, sliding the fish fingers from under the grill, he stopped suddenly and listened. He could hear the distant hiss and trickle of the refilling cistern but surely he'd heard it flush too – while he was showering. He stood out in the hall to listen. His distant reflection watched him like a stranger; his nose prickled with apprehension. The last teeth sucking sound of the full cistern stopped; and then, sure enough, the toilet flushed again.

"Who's there?" he shouted, bolstered to hear his own loud voice.

"Is someone there?" he called out again. Adrenalin suffused him. Fight overcame flight. He picked up a poker and almost ran towards the children's toilets. The cistern was still filling. He jammed up against the cubicle door just in case it closed on him. Then he held his hand millimetres below the chain-pull handle. The cistern squirted, spat and was finally silent. Suddenly he felt the first tiny touch of the chain-ring sinking onto his palm, then it lay over on its side and the descending chain formed a little mound of links within it. Higher and higher grew the little pile of links until 'whoosh': the cistern released its contents. At that he jumped onto the lavatory bowl and lifting the cistern lid began to poke and stab at its inner workings. Stabbing and pulling and shaking it as though it were a blameful sentient thing. Then he stood down, stretched his palm once more under the chain just when the cistern was almost full, and waited. He was shaking; palm outstretched like a child waiting for the lash of a cane.

Nothing happened. He waited a full two minutes and still nothing touched his hand. A burst of exultation took him and he stormed up the long hall between the gaping mirrors swinging the poker as though leathering some terrified intruder from his home.

He was too fired up to eat; headed straight for the village instead. And that night he did get drunk and sang too – regrettably.

It was a beautiful night, moonless but with the uncountable stars weighing down the see-through fabric of spacetime and when, still half cut, he got home, he lay on a blanket in the overgrown garden to watch them. He was cold when he woke. And a strange dream about tiny clusters of energy queuing in the universe for their mortal suits dissipated before he could fix it in memory.

Later facing the glimmering coals on his classroom mattress in the half-reality before deeper sleep, he felt something small and cold enter his bed and take shelter behind him.

In the second week of November the long Indian summer broke. Cold winds and then showers, a vengeful coup, swept the complacent leaves from the tossing trees and bushes. They skittered, dry as cornflakes, then clung saturated to the roads.

Almost unnoticed his heart had all but healed. He had a renewed swell of longing for the sensuality of women. Thoughts of the future regained importance. Certain old 'get on with it' certainties re-asserted precedence. He was running low on money. He found a job back in the city.

On his last night in the schoolhouse having bid farewell to his neighbours and all his friends in 'Jurr's', a little drunker than usual; all essential accoutrements packed in the boot of the car he'd bought with a tax-rebate, he lay bookless and lampless facing the blazing hearth to the sound of gusts lashing showers against the big windows; watching the light shows car headlights played on the walls; familiar shadows leaping to the rhythm of the flames.

On the cusp of deeper sleep he sensed the cold, small entity slip in behind him once again, steal a little warmth and snuggle down to rest. He was tempted to look back but he knew he'd see nothing. Nothing but his own supine shadow moving on the closed partition that separated his chamber from the other side.

Two Lies for the Prize of None

Jody Callahan

They showed up with Bill gone, like they sensed our land unguarded. The dog keeps going to the window to bark. I hoped it was nothing, that Wild was abusing the freedom I gave her to use her voice inside the house. After days of barking, though, she's broken me down. 'Cause of arthritis in my shoulder, I leave her leash behind. "If I get eaten by a bear," I tell Wild, "it's your fault." Like the dog would care.

I've been giving Wild walks on the bike path instead of patrolling our woods like I'm supposed to, 'cause of rumors of a black bear with cubs. If a bear is going from the Mill River or the wildlife sanctuary for a dumpster in town, it could amble through our acres. Bill likes to remind me that the homeless of Western Mass are more dangerous than bears. And, he tells me, Wild is a good bear detector. Sure, Wild would give her life to save him from a bear, but there's no guarantee she'd do it for me. Unless Bill told her to. Then she'd do it.

One of our *No Trespassing* signs is on the ground, a boot print muddying the words. Wild stops to sniff it and shoots me a look. She and Bill have that in common, pointing out the obvious like I don't have eyes that work. Next is a *No Camping* sign torn from a maple and thrown on some shrubs. Wild stands on hind legs to get the scent off of that one. Ahead, another sign, face down in the dirt. To repost means three trees will get another four nails. Sap will run from the holes. Bill says trees are tough and can take it. But just 'cause something can withstand a punch doesn't mean it won't hurt.

We defend the land ourselves – Bill says only suckers rely on local blue in a town hijacked by liberals. I'm licensed to carry but Bill forbids me to do so, alone, due to my emotional nature and lack of self-control. Legally, you can shoot a trespasser that crosses the threshold of your house, you just gotta say you feared for your life. But if threatened on your land out-of-doors, we owners have a fucked-up legal duty to retreat. The signs do protect us against injury claims, like say a junkie trips on a tree stump and lawyers-up looking for easy cash. But the signs probably won't scare off first-timers from coming into our woods to shoot up and drink. Those that get caught, receive a talking-to from Bill and Wild. No one returns for a second meeting with Wild. She's a hundred and forty pounds of muscle, under fur the color of highway snow. And when she's focused on someone, that fur stands on end, making her look unhinged. You needn't worry about Wild, though, long as you follow Bill's rules; she'll only attack on his command. Bill trained Wild when he was active duty. She served a few tours with two more handlers – one's currently deployed with a younger dog and the other shot himself, soon after getting home from Iraq. Bill says we got lucky, him ending up with first dibs on Wild in her retirement.

Wild's snout lifts in the air two beats before I catch on. It smells like skunk. Not animal but weed. The scent always takes me back to my wasted years, living on a commune, cross country in the Northwest. Bill thinks I'm too chicken to walk the woods regularly with him and Wild, but it's more than bears. Woods make me funny – like homesick. On the commune I lived deep among trees. When the group went belly-up, leaving me rootless, I went to a church for free meals, and there they straightened my path.

Longing for youth is useless so I stay out of the woods, much as I can. But after patrolling with Bill, Wild sprawls on the floor like a bear skin rug and gives off an odor of earth and pine. Every time I vacuum, I think the same thought: dirt's got to be removed even when it smells clean.

Tree trunks marked with dark paint, the color of congealed blood, arrow toward a tent. Hooked low on a branch hangs one of our signs flipped to the blank side and spray painted: *Deadhead Way.*

Bill's in Texas consulting for a defense contractor. It's not nice to think, but it's a vacation when he's gone. I sleep. I eat. I'll complete my chores but do them when I want – which is right before he's expected back. The dog's devastated, of course. I've tried to get Wild on the couch to get on her good side, but the dog won't oblige and gives me a look of pity or disappointment. It's made me wonder if the Buddhists with their reincarnation stuff got it right. Wild is like a Cavalry Scout wearing a dog suit. Watching me. Ready to report back to the boss.

"Whoa." Kids sitting on a milk crate jump. He has one of those well-trimmed beards, popular with his generation. Both of them are young and white. The girl wears an updated version of my old garb – flowered skirt, hiking boots, and dreadlocked dirty-blonde hair. If they hadn't trespassed on the land, and I'd seen them sitting under a sign declaring *Deadhead Way* I would've laughed. These kids haven't been on earth long enough to hear Jerry play live.

"Is it a wolf or a dog?" the boy asks. Wild corners him against the tent, her tail erect, and her fur agitated.

"Wolf's in her blood," I lie.

"Does she bite?" the girl asks. The girl could be my granddaughter if I had a granddaughter that lost her way.

"Bites if I tell her to. You're on private property."

"You the owner?" she asks.

"Move on before everyone comes out," I say, as if I have ready backup instead of an empty house. "And take everything. Don't be leaving your rubbish behind. Careful!" I warn, as the boy reaches out to Wild. But Wild takes something from his hand. Beef jerky. She wags her tail. Traitorous bitch.

"A Peak bar is basically a dog treat." The girl has the nerve to smile.

I know Peak bars. Made from grass-fed beef and organic, cranberry-eating wild turkeys. When I found out how much a box cost, I took another sample of the turkey one offered at Stop & Shop, and said I'd think about it. No way I'd throw money around for expensive packaging of ingredients I can raise myself.

"That's a high-ticket dog treat," I say to the girl. "Hey, how long it take you to grow those dreads?" Curiosity of her hair gets me before I remember not to make small talk with trespassers. Her dreadlocks are so long, it looks like she must've started as a toddler. In my time, a lot of us hippie-white-girls had them. It's unusual for our color, today, I think. And hers are smooth and tight. Maybe they're done different now.

"They're not real," the girl laughs. "They're extensions." She pulls a section to the front and strokes it, like it's a pet. "I might have them taken out because everybody's doing it. It's lost originality."

The kids are frauds! Slumming it. Up close I see the tent and gear is clean and expensive. Even their boots haven't been broken in, still buffed with manufacturer's polish. It reminds me of graffiti I've seen on the bike path bridge, *Kill All Trustys,* probably sprayed by a real street person. Now I don't condone public defacement or murderous threats coming from those who refuse to straighten their path, but I do feel a bit of solidarity with that graffiti-writer. I remember it myself. Coming from nothing. Having nothing. And some money-child would join to live in the woods, and bail when they couldn't stand the smell of themselves unwashed.

"I thought locs would be easier on this... adventure. Nothing has gone right." The girl waves toward a line of gorgeous pines, like the trees are at fault for her displeasure. "There are ticks! And it's dangerous without doors and walls. You never know who could be sneaking around."

"It's not that bad," the boy corrects her to me. "She's always exaggerating."

"You were just complaining about the mosquitoes," she says. "And our stomachs have been upset since day one. I knew we should have taken a class on the outdoors. We need guidance on how to do this right."

"You using water purification tablets?" I ask. "Sprayed your gear with permethrin? And DEET daily, right?"

She shakes her head and speaks like she's repeating words she's at odds with believing. "We want to be natural. They didn't use chemicals in the olden days."

I look to Wild to roll my eyes, but she's too busy feasting on their meat. "How old they live to in the olden days?" I say.

Neither kid answers, like I'm intruding in their spat. They snap at each other, get in their digs; it's obvious they've been arguing for days. These two could teach a course on bad camping: keep your stake lines slack, tent under dead branches, and travel with someone you hate.

"They didn't even put up the rain fly," I tell the trees since no one else is listening to a word I say. It's frustrating with pampered kids like this – is it ignorance or laziness that makes them this way?

"I wish she could come with us," the girl loud-whispers to the boy. "I'd feel safer with her around." She piles her hair into a big knot at the top of her head, and not trusting it will hold, stands limbs raised and open-palmed, reminding me of that Hindu God with all the arms.

My mind flips. My bones relax. The girl's invitation spreads through me easy, like the doctor's pill I take when sunk too low. Being poor isn't a crime and neither should the luck of being born rich. She's like an apparition brought forth to show a possibility I forgot exists. I can almost feel the ache of sleeping on uneven earth again, the vivid dreams that living outside will bring.

"Yeah, but she'd have to be on a leash," the boy says, feeding Wild more of the bar, and smoothing down her fur. "We wouldn't want her to run off."

Nobody can see inside me, to know I'd mistaken myself for a dog. Still, I feel a fool in front of them. In front of Wild. "You've an hour to break down. How much cash you got?"

"Why?" the girl asks.

"Spray painted my trees. Tore down my signs. Or should we call your parents?"

The boy shrugs like money is beneath him. The girl cries, of course. I've seen it before – those with few reasons to cry do it more than anyone else. Two hundred and forty dollars and I don't feel one penny bad; I spot a gold credit card in her pack.

"Crazy bitch," the girl mumbles, her bottom lip wobbles like a netted fish.

Heat prickles from deep inside and advances upward to my face. I twist, reaching behind my good hip. With my other hand, I lift a tangled mass of frizzy grays, and lay the metal barrel sideways, cooling the nape of my neck. Bill says never point a gun at anything you aren't prepared to lose. With the piece doing an unorthodox cooling job, the only thing I'm at risk of losing here is my head.

There was a mystic in the commune who claimed he could slow time. A pistol can do that too. I count beats in my chest followed by their innocent murmur: lubb-dupp swish, lubb-dupp swish, lubb-dupp swish. I feel a bead of sweat on the tip of my nose before it drops. And then another. The air still carries the scent of weed but I notice there's something sweet too – like honeysuckle or jasmine around. And with a breeze reaching in from the direction of the trail I came from, there's something dark and musty, like a disgruntled bear awoken from sleep and heading this way.

The boy's breathing is fast and shallow. The girl's eyes have lost whatever color they were, looking like wet golf balls in her head. Urine begins its bond with dirt, making a mud puddle between her boots.

"What size are your feet?" I ask.

"Why?" she says.

"Just tell her, stupid!" the boy screams.

True to her nature, the dog won't side with the weak. Wild abandons meat offerings to investigate smaller prey in the darkness behind the tent. Warning clicks from chipmunks herald Wild's arrival.

"Seven and a half," the girl sobs. "Are you stealing my boots? What will I wear?" Bill says females talk too much, and in this moment, I tend to agree.

The boy pummels a fist into his other hand like a frustrated catcher waiting for a ball. The girl flinches, and I see how it is.

I want to slap her.

And hold her.

And encourage her to run.

"Lucky you," I say. "Your boots are too small." Two lies for the prize of none.

I tell the kids again they've got an hour, gesturing the gun towards his private parts for fun. Still, I keep my shoulders squared leaving the tent, and pivot to the rush of movement behind me; I learned long ago how to sidestep a blow. But it isn't the kids. It's Wild back on duty, chaperoning me home.

It's been a few weeks and the kids are famous now. All over TV. She went missing, first. Happened a few counties over from here. He hightailed it before her days-old body was found by a hiker, off trail looking for a squatting spot 'cause nature had called.

Reporters have been repeating that strangulation is the most common form of violence between committed couples right now; suffocation was more popular in the past. Occasionally, someone will remember to ask about other missing girls, ones that aren't cute and white and blond. Is anyone looking for them? But those girls get forgotten quick when new details about the white kids are released.

Former classmates are asked for their insight. Was there any indication this would happen? Was he possessive? She compliant? Were there any signs?

The boy will be found sooner or later, dead or alive, that part doesn't much interest me. Since meeting the kids, there are other things I've been sorting inside my head.

Bill wants to know what's happened to make me friends with Wild. I play dumb and don't say about the variety pack of Peak bars we're splurging on. There's a lot he doesn't know.

Planning is quiet and carefully done. It could happen during Bill's next trip. Or the next. I could go a few hours after he leaves, but there's Wild to consider. She'd be locked inside for days.

I'm careful to temper my excitement. It's a good thing Wild can't speak in words – Bill says she's got the prance of pre-deployment in her paws. He's wondering if she's got dog dementia, the way she's acting so strange. It's like Wild knows what I'm going to do before I've decided it's so; I know it'd be crazy to take her. No one will remember an old lady like me – but an old lady running wild in the woods with a massive dog, now that would be an interesting story to tell.

Avocado
Laura Morris

The first thing I stole was an avocado. The dark fruit looked like sleeping nestlings tucked into the brown packing paper, and I remember scanning the green cardboard tray for the largest. It wasn't the darkest in the tray, but it was the largest. Shaped like a pear, heavier than an egg, the hard shell felt so cool beneath my fingertips as I slipped it into the deep of my duffel coat pocket.

I walked home quickly, a little giddy, feeling as though my torso was trying to move faster than my legs. When I turned the corner into my street and saw Sara from next door, I closed my eyes, hoping she wouldn't recognise me beneath my hood, but she did, and stopped to talk. I took parcels in for Sara and Marty when they were at work. I didn't know what was inside the brown cardboard boxes, and often shook them, trying to guess. Sara was saying things about the rain, and the noises in the lane at night. I knew it was just words, but the tune of her voice hurt my head. While she talked, I kept my right hand in my pocket, stroking the avocado with my thumb, and when her voice became shrill, I pressed hard on the shell. I liked that she didn't know what I was doing, inside my pocket. When the rain came heavier, and Sara left, I studied my hand: green flesh under my fingernails, and in the skin of the avocado were the scars of five tiny crescent moons.

Cutting the avocado open with a knife, halving it, and making a meal from it seemed wrong after that. And so, when I got it home, I crushed the fruit in my hand, until the skin caved into the meat. I scooped out the stone and nibbled at the flesh that was still attached, allowing it to slide between my fingers. The avocado was ripe, and each green curl was buttery and smooth. I didn't remove the tiny little green sticker. I didn't pull down my hood. I sat there, legs crossed on the cold tiled floor, eating, and once finished, I wiped my greasy fingers on the bottom of my duffel coat. I had never tasted an avocado before, and had only ever seen the inside of one on the television. It was rich and nutty and good.

On Sundays I caught the number 19 bus to Canton to visit Debbie. She helped me fill in forms. Sometimes I took groceries she asked me to pick up from the corner shop.

How much do I owe you? she asked, when I handed over a small block of cheese. Nothing, I said. I stole it.

Right, she said, adding that she didn't believe me, that I wouldn't be brave enough.

She opened the cupboard above the kettle, where she kept her money in a chipped teacup, took out three pound coins, and handed them to me. I pushed them around the table, while she lit a cigarette from the grill, and opened the back door, blowing the smoke towards the wheelie bin. After finishing, she stubbed out the cigarette on a saucer, took a chopping board from a drawer, a knife from the draining board, and began to cut the cheese thinly, arranging it on sliced white bread, before putting it under the heat. Once cooked, she handed me the plate, and I stared at the fat forming like tears on top of the melted cheese. I picked off the sliced tomatoes, leaving them on the side of the plate. The poor little pips were drowning in their own juice.

Later, when I got home, I stacked the three pound coins on the coffee table. *I have earned them; I should use them for something significant,* I remember thinking, but two days later when the electricity meter started beeping before my money arrived, I put the coins in my duffel coat pocket and topped up the plastic white card at the corner shop.

Before I stole a bottle of nail varnish from the chemist across the road, I spent a long time turning the tiny glass bottles upside down, and reading the names on the bottom. I said each one out loud – *Vamp, Kitten, Stiletto,* then opened each of the tester bottles, trying out the colours on a piece of card hanging from the display. I chose *Roulette. Ladies and gentleman, place your bets.* I painted my nails in my bedroom, leaning on a large brown envelope from the DWP that I didn't want to open. The left hand was easier than the right, but I took my time. I had plenty of time. Exactly a week later, I went back, and stole the matching lipstick, and at home, in the mirror, I practised applying it, then removing it with a square of toilet roll. The lipstick was a dark plum colour, almost black in the light of my bathroom, like a freshly formed bruise.

My nails and lips done, I climbed onto the toilet seat, and looked out of the small window above the cistern and down into Sara and Marty's garden. There were brightly coloured plastic toys, a blue paddling pool, a small barbecue near the shed. There was a large wooden rabbit hutch on stubby little legs. Its door was open, and the two children were playing with a white rabbit on the grass. The scene looked like an advert from a mail order catalogue, and I thought of all the parcels I took in for them. There were boxes and packets stacked up in my hallway at Christmas, waiting for Sara to collect.

Saturdays were the hardest. Those empty days of hollow hours to fill, and no live TV with women chatting to structure my day. At One Stop I spent twenty minutes reading the stories on the front of magazines – MY HUSBAND MARRIED MY NANNY! MY PARTNER RAN OFF WITH MY DAUGHTER! 15 KIDS AND COUNTING! I didn't pick up the magazines because the woman behind the counter with the knitted jumper and glasses on a beaded string was watching me. I watched her too, and when she turned around to reach a card of batteries for a customer, I looked in the fridge for something I could take. Between the pints of milk and cartons of flavoured yogurts was a single can of squirty cream. There was a picture of a strawberry on the front, digitally altered and made to look like a face. It had eyebrows, eyes and a mouth, as if drawn on with the cream. I picked it up and tucked the can into the sleeve of my coat. It was cool against my skin, and I shivered. Once out of the shop and on the street, I slid the can out and into my hand. I walked down a lane behind the shops so no one could see me, crouched behind an industrial bin, shook the can, removed the lid, and squirted the cream into my mouth. It tasted like a trip Debbie had taken me on years ago. We had gone on a coach. I don't remember where we were going that day or why, just that sweet taste on my tongue.

I continued the walk home, and tried to concentrate on stepping one foot in front of the other, but I had the taste of cream in my mouth, and couldn't think about anything else. I didn't wait to pass a lane and squirted from the can onto my tongue in the middle of the street. I stood in front of a charity shop window, peered in, and did it again, meeting the eyes of a customer framed by old leather boots and strings of fake pearls. I took too much that time, and the cream expanded in the small cave of my mouth, like that yellow foam they use to fill in cavities in walls. I couldn't contain it and opened my mouth, allowing the cream to ooze out, and run down my lips. The customer watched me, and her mouth opened, and made a shape, as if appalled by what I was doing. I continued to walk, and took more and more until eventually the cream stopped squirting, and just a sweet liquid trickled out. Then I sucked at the nozzle.

Stealing the wrapping paper was easy. I found the cheapest thing in the shop – a packet of Orbit chewing gum – and paid for it at the self-service till, but kept the roll of paper tucked under my arm, instead of scanning it through. Once out of the shop I placed the wrapping paper in my tote bag, and carried the bag on my shoulder. Walking down St Mary Street, I could feel someone tapping me on the back. I turned around, expecting to see a security guard, but it was just the roll of paper brushing against me as I walked. I laughed to myself about that, although there was a part of me that wanted to be stopped. I didn't have the answers, but I wanted the questions.

Afterwards, with two pellets of spearmint chewing gum in my mouth, I stole a scented candle from one of the department stores in the shopping centre. I carried it in both hands, went down the escalator with it, and walked out of the automatic doors, expecting an alarm to go off. I even paused for a moment, but nothing happened. Later, before I caught the bus, I went into the pub and used the toilets downstairs. After I had peed, I stayed on the toilet, my knickers still round my ankles. I reached for my tote bag, took out the paper, and removed its cellophane wrapper. I tore off a corner of the paper, and wrapped it around the candle. I didn't have any sticky tape, so I scrunched the paper together at the top and shoved it into the bag. I left the roll of wrapping paper in the toilet cubicle, propped behind the sanitary bin. When I took the candle to Debbie for her birthday, she unwrapped it, and sniffed it suspiciously.

Too sweet, she said. It will give me a headache.

The last time I visited her, the candle was still next to the TV, the price sticker on its side, and the pale wax growing a layer of grime.

I had never cycled on the road before, only around the streets by the flats where I grew up, but after a phonecall from the DWP, I took a bike from outside the pub. I knew how to ride the bike, but I didn't understand the roads, and men inside big silver cars kept beeping their horns at me. I cycled to the next village and stopped outside the small post office, leaning the bike against the wall. I scanned the stationery and chose a child's writing set, sliding it beneath my duffel coat. I rode home, leaving the bike in the lane. I opened the writing set and counted out the twenty sheets of paper and twenty envelopes. Each sheet was decorated with a cartoon monkey, lion and elephant. I took a poetry book I'd been given at secondary school from the shelf in the living room, and began copying out the poems, stealing famous lines, signing them with my signature. It took a long time, as I had twenty sheets of paper to use, and I had to be careful to use my best handwriting, and to spell all the words correctly. Later I posted the poems through the letter boxes of the houses by the church. The small houses with the red bricks, not the big houses with the grey bricks.

Yes, I had taken, but I was also giving back.

All I wanted was the feeling I'd had when I stole the avocado. I'd tried stealing them since: riper ones, larger ones, but I couldn't get that same tingle to creep over my arms, until early one morning, when I knew Sara, Marty and the kids would still be asleep, I climbed over my garden wall and into their garden. I could hear cars in the distance, making their way into the city, but the street was quiet. I unbolted the hutch that sat on the lawn and lifted out the rabbit. It struggled, kicking me in my belly.

Shh, I said softly. Come on now. There, there.

I couldn't climb back over the wall with the rabbit in my arms, so I held it close to my chest, unlocked the garden gate, and walked through, into the lane. There were empty cans and burned rubbish from where the gang gathered on weekends. New graffiti on a garage door shouted FUCK THE TORIES!

Back in my garden, I placed the rabbit on the grass. Stay, I said to it, because I had to climb over the wall to bolt Sara's gate, before climbing back into my garden, but the rabbit didn't stay like I had told it and hid beneath a rose bush. After I had got down on my hands and knees to pull it out, my arms were scratched from the thorns, and dots of blood appeared.

I got the rabbit into the house, but I wasn't sure what to do with it after that. I held it on my lap, but it kept trying to get away from me. I dug my nails into its belly, but its blue eyes looked frightened.

Some people say all babies are born with blue eyes, but I know that's not true.

I made myself a cup of black tea and sat on the sofa, watching the rabbit hop around, hoping it would eventually settle. It went from room to room, leaving small black droppings in the bathroom and hallway. I swept them into a dustpan then shook them into the kitchen bin.

I ignored the children's cries coming from next door's garden and ignored their stammering knocks on my front door. An hour later a piece of paper came through my letter box. The note was written in red crayon, and said HAV YoU SEEn OuR RaBiT? I sighed, folded the note in half then turned it into a paper aeroplane. I flew it around the living room, making whirring noises until I got tired and lay down on the floor. I stared at the light bulb hanging from the middle of the ceiling until it hurt my eyes, and then I closed them. When I woke up, I saw that the rabbit had chewed through the cord of the vacuum cleaner.

We both needed to eat. My fridge only contained three eggs and half a jar of jam, and I didn't think the rabbit would like either of those, and so I went out to get the animal some food.

At the pet shop, when the assistant was busy helping a woman choose fish, I took a bag of rabbit food. It was a large bag, too large to stuff beneath my coat, so I took it quickly, held it behind my back as I left the shop, and made my way home. Sara's children were playing on their scooters in the street. I felt them stare as I passed them, swinging the bag of rabbit food from my hand.

When I got home, I couldn't find the rabbit. I didn't like that it could hide places and I didn't know where it was. Eventually, I found it behind the sofa, but I knew I needed to keep it contained. In the garden were planks of old wood, left there by the previous tenant. I arranged them in the kitchen, creating some sort of pen, and put down a towel for it to sleep on. I filled the bowl I ate cereal from with water and poured out some of the rabbit food onto a saucer. It ate and drank and even allowed me to stroke it, to tickle its belly.

Most evenings now, I sit with the rabbit, telling it stories about when I was young, although I can't remember all the details, just feelings mostly – feelings and smells, the way things tasted. Autumn is coming. The evenings are getting colder. The smell of bonfire hangs in the air. The rabbit sits on its hind legs. Its ears are up, alert to the smallest crumb of sound, while its eyes – round, anxious, and fixed on the back door – seem to be planning escape.

Things We Did While Waiting for (Good) News

Lenore Myka

We made lists, for one thing. Of groceries, primarily.

Whole milk

Brown eggs

Unsalted butter

Plum tomatoes

Skin-on chicken thighs

Panda paws ice cream

Kettle chips

Chardonnay

We ordered online, did curbside pickup at Wegman's, giving the delivery person a thumbs up, shouting through tightly closed windows *Thank you so much!* As if pushing a cart to the curb was an act of extreme heroism. Most things, in those days, seemed to be.

"Do we tip them?" I asked James the first time we went.

"Doesn't that defeat the purpose?"

"Why would we ever go into a store again?" said he, a Myers-Briggs INFJ.

He once told me less than three percent of the population constituted this most rare of personality types. I'll get you a medal, I'd said, but the truth was I liked that he was a rare species, having traveled all this way with me. *Most people wouldn't have,* most people reminded me. Discovering him made me special too.

"We'd go into a store because we could."

I knew the first thing my mother would do once Dad came home (if he came home) and we'd left was go grocery shopping. She'd slip into her fleece-lined boots, dab her lips with Maybelline's coral reef, and search for her purse, which she was constantly misplacing.

That was another thing we did: searched for things my mother misplaced. A purse, a phone charger, the walnuts she'd roasted for a coffeecake she hoped to bake, the recipe for the coffeecake, the planner where she recorded hospital updates.

"She's always losing things," I told my sister while out walking the dog.

"Well that's nothing new. She's been losing things as long as we've been alive."

I shifted the phone so I could revive my frozen fingers in my coat pocket. I'd been in town less than three weeks and had already lost a mitten, presumably dropping it in the Tully's parking lot where James and I had gotten takeout sandwiches after discovering my parents' favorite spot for Friday night fish fry was, like so many other places, permanently closed.

I didn't tell my sister I'd been losing things too.

"It's different this time."

"How so?"

I couldn't say. Maybe it wasn't that her forgetfulness was different but that my expectations were. We were having a crisis. I wanted her—I wanted *me*—to rise to it. It wasn't enough that we survived this war; I wanted to be a member of the resistance.

The bachelor brothers across the street baked Italian Christmas cookies. I called those brothers Larry, brother Daryl, and other brother Daryl, which I thought my father, had he been with us, would've found hilarious. We consumed those cookies, chardonnay, and kettle chips from the couch where we watched *Jeopardy!* each evening.

All of those episodes were prerecorded in October. Alex Trebek died in November. It was now December. James rarely volunteered answers, but my mother and I competed, especially when the category was 19th Century American Poets or Famous Female British Novelists. *Virginia Woolf!* we'd cry. *George Eliot!* But our answers were inadmissible without *Who is---?*

"It's hard to believe he's dead, isn't it?" said my mother.

I startled. "Who?"

"*Him,* of course. Who did you think I was talking about?"

Breath returned, I studied the TV. Alex *did* appear very much alive, delighted as he was by the twenty-four-year-old from Nevada. That kid started slow, barely hitting the buzzer the first five minutes of airtime. But a switch inside would go off and—wham!—the board was his.

By air and by sea for five hundred, Alex. Gastronomical explorations for a thousand.

He intuited daily doubles, wagering high, feigning uncertainty, his tell a mouth twist barely suppressing glee.

Months later, I read this kid had died of undisclosed causes.

"Suicide?" said James.

Wasn't that what *undisclosed causes* meant?

On a particularly bad day, James suggested I take a bath, which reminded me of the Raymond Carver story.

I wanted to reread that story, but my parents didn't have any Carver in the house and I forgot to look online. And then I wondered how much I actually wanted to read it, because I knew what the ending of the story implied, and I couldn't think about that.

I did not take a bath.

We recorded a lot of death. Impending deaths, like my father's cousin who had pancreatic cancer, but also the larger, public deaths. I kept track of the daily national count: 267,000; 333,000; 400,000. The international count was inconceivable.

Afterward, no matter the time of day, I went to bed.

We hoped Dad would be home by Christmas. We hoped he'd be home on Christmas.

Sometimes the dog paced the rooms of the house, whining and sniffing and looking at me beseechingly, searching for something, for someone he wouldn't find. Only I noticed this. I never reported to the others about it.

We told each other stories. Or rather, my mother told stories, we listened. They were stories I'd heard countless times, stories I knew well, stories I'd lived.

"Remember that vacation to New York during the transit strike? Remember that time you broke your arm horseback riding?"

Yes, I'd say. Yes.

"Remember that time at the beach when the dolphin followed you? Which reminds me: take those crystal dolphins when you leave. Take the old coffeemaker. You want it, right?"

I did not reply. To agree to take anything felt perilous. I would not agree until I knew more.

"We've had our moments, your father and I," my mother said. "I won't say it's been perfect."

This was another particularly bad day when, in addition to calling the hospital, we called funeral parlors, cemeteries.

"We had a good marriage."

Did she say *had* or *we've had* or *we have*? I counted the number of times the grammar or tense was wrong. I started writing in pencil, carrying an eraser.

We reported on the life we saw through the kitchen windows. A hawk hunting field mice. A red fox. That sweet neighbor, Hope, walking her three-legged rescue.

Once, four bucks strolled through the dead grass, pausing to rub their hindquarters against bare saplings. One lifted his tail, releasing a stream of pebbly shit. I counted the piles of shit on the lawn, and the holes dug at the side of the house. Six piles. Seven holes. I wrote notes to my father about this.

Rabbits are living in your flowerbed, or maybe moles.

The deer practically ring the doorbell! They destroyed your coconut coir doormat.

I slipped these notes into the mailbox, lifting the little red flag so the mail carrier would know to pick something up. Doing so was satisfying in a way the rest of my life during that time was not.

Sometimes I delivered these notes to the hospital myself, along with slices of the coffeecake my mother had finally recovered the recipe for and my father's electric shaver. James waited in the no parking zone while I pulled up my mask and ran into the lobby, stood in front of a tablet that beamed a green light onto my forehead, logged in my name and the floor my father was on, which was constantly changing. Fourth. Ninth. Thirteenth. Twelfth.

Sometimes, I wondered if I could make a break for it before security stopped me. Sometimes I wondered if I could don a white lab coat and an air of importance and stride up to the elevators without notice. Always, afterward, I'd cross the street and stand on the sidewalk and look up to what I thought might be the fourth/ninth/thirteenth/twelfth floor.

"Hello, Dad," I'd say aloud. "Are you there? I love you I love you I love you I love you."

We hoped Dad would be home by New Year's. We hoped he'd be home on New Year's.

I wrote in a drugstore notebook, never losing it but once, when James needed paper, which we were always looking for and could never find. This was a mystery because my parents kept copious handwritten notes, my father especially.

His handwriting was everywhere. By the basement light switch (*Remember to turn off the lights!*); on the back of the basement door (*Did you remember to turn off the lights?*); on the calendar by the telephone (*cardiologist, electric bill, C's birthday, tennis, meals-on-wheels*); on the refrigerator door (a quote circled "Old age is a privilege denied many," and a reminder *duly noted!!!*).

On another evening walk I told my sister: "His stuff is everywhere."

"I know."

"He's everywhere in that house."

"I know."

"It's so difficult to see it. I want to cry, or run."

"I know."

We reminded each other to eat something, to brush our teeth, to breathe.

My mother ordered a new television. My parents had complained about their old one for years. They couldn't get the remote to work with the cable box or the cable box to work with the remote. They had too many remotes—for the volume, the cable, the analogue TV, the streaming services, some of which they could only watch on an even older television in the basement. They had a repairman—a Russian or Slovak, Vlad or Yuri—come over to fix it. But I wouldn't allow anyone inside the house.

"Why *not*?" my mother roared. "It's *my* house!"

"Mom!" I said. "*Why* is Dad in the hospital?"

We picked up the new television (curbside). James set it up. The remote worked with the cable, and then it didn't, and my mom fretted about what my father would say when he finally got home, so much fretting that James spent a weekend figuring out what the problem was. Eventually, he got that new remote to work again, at which point my mother burst into tears.

I thought we'd binge-watch shows. But it was hard to concentrate beyond a half-hour episode of *Jeopardy!*.

Still, the television was always on. I avoided it. So often it was the news, or public service announcements or advertisements about the news. Always the message was the same and who wanted to be reminded of what we were living every day, every hour, every minute?

Unless we were calling the hospital, we also avoided the telephone. It was usually someone asking questions, making suggestions, as if we weren't *in the trenches* as my mother called it, as if we'd *never thought to ask* countless questions or to find out if it was *really* impossible to visit Dad in the hospital.

When we did answer, I could hear the relief in the voices whenever I said I had to go. They, like us, couldn't wait to get off the phone.

On Christmas Eve, buoyed by some not bad news, we rallied. James got champagne and I put up a small artificial tree and my mother prepared her famous cheeseball. We ate in front of the fireplace, resting our feet on the coffee table while snow buffeted the windows and the dog wedged himself between us.

Eventually, we made calls not only to the hospital's nurses and doctors, but to my father himself. Initially, the calls were clocked in seconds, but over time they grew.

I recorded these calls in my notebook until they got too long and repetitive, the substance of which was that my father was better than anyone else seemed to realize and he wanted to come home yesterday.

"Remember that guy from *Jeopardy!*," James said once we'd returned home, "the one we watched with your mom?"

I nodded.

"It wasn't suicide."

"What then?"

"Complications from surgery."

I shuddered. In a way, that was worse. He was, after all, only twenty-four. My father would be eighty-four in April, god-willing. Where was the justice in that?

"After everything we've been through and you talk about justice?! Aren't you *glad*?"

"Of course I'm glad!"

What I didn't say: I would have made a deal with the devil if it had ever come to that.

The last thing I did before I left was pick Dad up from the hospital. He sat in the front passenger's seat beside me, gaunt and smaller than I remembered him being, blinking away tears.

"I thought I was never gonna get out of that place," he said.

"I thought I was gonna die in that place," he said.

"I probably will die in that place," he said.

"But not yet," I said.

He turned his face toward me and smiled. Then he squinted through the windshield.

"My, but the world looks beautiful."

It was the middle of January in upstate New York. Gray, bitter, the sun's feeble attempts at revelation only made the sky jaundiced, sickly. Mounds of icy, smog-infested snow teetered on street corners. A homeless man wearing a down jacket held together with duct-tape and pushing a shopping cart filled with black plastic bags gave us the finger as we drove past.

I reached across the console and squeezed my father's warm hand. I couldn't have agreed more.

Primal Cuts
Catriona Shine

I start the mincer, and its trundle pauses my customers' talk. This is my time for hashed reflection. I'm not alone-alone, and it's only for a while. I'm in for the long haul with what the cold room cost me.

I pass the mouth of the plastic bag through the tape machine and plump its round weight into a carrier bag.

How's that for you, Susie?

Lovely. Drop over with Ludo when he comes down. We had a lovely time on our trip to Rome, didn't we Fran?

It was fabulous. I'll take three big slices of bacon, Alma, when you're ready. Match this evening. They're always looking for players—boys and girls—if your lads are interested. When will they be down?

Within a month, we hope.

I give them this assurance, though it's not hope I'm feeling. I'm feeling odd, wide-eyed. I'm beginning to see the edges of myself.

Susie and Fran head up to the primary school together, their shopping out of the way before the school day even starts. The shop is empty.

Before I opened, I put a notice in the local newsletter, introducing myself, mentioning my grand-aunt's bakery, so they wouldn't think I was some outsider trying to sell them foreign meat. My customers are better than any club and not everyone comes to my shop, but those that do talk about those that don't.

In the this-way-that-way gusts of words, I see the reason everyone's been warning me about those Sullivans. They know the easy prey I'll be to the youngest, a prime specimen of raw north Kerry sex. The curls alone. The arms alone. The eyebrows.

I already knew all about him when he first came in, so it was hard not to say, Patrick, how're you getting on with the filly? but he laughed when I told him my name.

You're the one with the horses, I said, to redeem myself.

He eyed my mincer.

You're the French one, he said. Should I be worried for my fillies?

I told him my grandmother was French. No horsemeat here, I said. I'm on the lookout for a good source.

We both smiled, a tumbling-forward smile that was really a laugh with the sound implied, and the sun scorched dust onto my right cheek.

I stock Patrick Sullivan's potatoes. The large quantity of vegetables I have for sale is only ever mentioned in praise. This is the butcher's. I am the butcher, yet I bring in as much in veg as in meat. Not wanting to let the vegetables take over, I stack them by the window and on shelves along the wall opposite the counter. I have them on freestanding units too, and the onions and garlic hang from the ceiling, in dialogue with the cured hams that hover above me in the meat section. The counter stands in its original spot, having negotiated its position with the floor for half a century. Both agree: It must stay where it is unless I want to retile the floor and move the suspended lighting. The counter stays in the middle of the room, and I keep half the space to myself and my beautifully fragmented carcasses.

Vegetables sell on a weekly string of rumours, word of mouth about my floury potatoes, rhubarb bundles with slimmer, tastier stems than the supermarket, my ready-for-the-pot stew and stir-fry mixes. I've hit a chord with the single farmers and commuters. Good, generous portions of meat, veg and potatoes; fling it in the pot, the pan.

I know this shop. My grand-aunt's bakery was right across the street. Auntie Nell was skinny as they come, though she ate wonky meringues and burst tea cakes like they were popcorn. When her big-bellied son took over, he didn't last a month. Nell was notorious for baking without recipes. Keep adding until the texture is right, she would say to me, as I stood on a stool by the worktop. More, she'd say, more, easy, easy, that's it. Stop now. Stop.

Uncle Bob ate up the inventory and put a padlock on the door.

Whenever I was staying with Nell, I'd be sent over here with a list on an unused receipt. Maisie and Pat were always saying they were looking for an assistant just my size. How much was my auntie paying me, they wanted to know, and did I have any experience with a bandsaw. I was never sure if they were joking. As soon as they passed me the knotted plastic bag I took off. When my eyes latched onto the wedding cake on display in Nell's window I forgot about right and left and right again. I ran straight across the street in fear of Maisie and Pat, and I remember being taken aback when I looked through the window and saw my face smiling in the reflection.

I did think of opening a bakery, but I'm a bit of an Uncle Bob. I've a distant memory of Maisie's cleaver swooshing through air and hacking through flesh, and I want what Maisie had in that moment. I don't want anyone to be physically harmed, neither my equality-spouting ex-boss nor the male junior colleague who got my promotion. It's more akin to smashing a cup or punching a pillow, what I'm after. I want to be the one who owns the sharpest knives. I've never been squeamish but, until now, people had no way of knowing.

Patrick Sullivan.

I think it like that, his full name, spoken in my mind at regular intervals throughout the day, a what-is-he-up-to-now exhalation, and forgiveness there before I find out what he's done. I'll be alone here for two months at the very least. Ludo's project is on site, and there have been delays. The end of the school year is drawing close.

Fran, back again because she's always forgetting something: she knows exactly what I'm thinking when my eyes linger on her bag of amandine potatoes.

I'll give it to him, she says, he knows his spuds, young Sullivan. Keep that counter between you and him, that's all I'll say.

Fran's my best customer. They're good eaters, her crowd. Two of them are the same year at school as my dangly waifs. I wonder if they'll be friends. Cici and Angelo have vowed to make friends with no one. Cici's apparently not even going to look at them, however she'll manage it. I can't imagine anyone diverting their eyes from Fran Halloran.

When did you say your crowd are coming down, Alma? I was talking to Timmy Buckley there. He trains the under-fourteen boys.

Oh, it'll be June now, sure. They'd may as well see out the school year where they are.

They're good at school, I'd say, are they?

Well, now, if they'd study.

I'll make sure Prendergast puts them in the A classes with my lads. Right, let's see. Give me eight hundred grams of minced beef as well.

I exchange a lamb's leg and the scream of the saw for ten chops and begin to scrape fatty sawdust off the glossy flesh. The bell jingles, and Patrick Sullivan with his sack of spuds steps through the door.

Lovely, I say, put them down there by the others.

He comes back with two more, one over each shoulder, and I hold the door for him. I'm not one for romance novels but this is the kind of Mick-flick hunk my mind would conjure up if the details were scant.

There's something I need to show you upstairs, I say.

He laughs.

We've been doing this every time he comes in, which is once or twice a week, ever since Stuart the dentist said, in front of us both, Watch out for this one, Alma. He has fangs.

You've had me up all night, says Patrick. I don't have another round in me.

I might catch you this evening then, I say, when I get back from the presbytery.

Jesus, he says.

He's next.

I thought it was my horses you were after.

Where do you think you are, France? We'd have to disguise your old nags as beef.

I have no nags, he says, not smiling anymore.

There was a line I hadn't seen, concealed as it was in the non-porno part of our conversation. I go back to the carnivorous side of the counter, skewer his receipt and ring up the price of three sacks of potatoes.

What about Samsara, I say, will she be ready for Listowel?

She'll run, he says, but I'm not counting on a win.

She's a beautiful mare.

First outing. As long as she isn't injured, I'll be happy.

Does it happen often?

Always the optimist, he says, eyeing the cleaver I absentmindedly picked up.

I can't rightly explain it, but I love the weight of that cleaver in my hand. I love the name of it. I love the generous proportion of blade to handle. There's power in a knife, even with no threat at all.

What has you so riled? he says, and then Susie Casey's mother comes in. Her own name evades me.

It says you're closed for lunch, she says, but I saw you there. Are you open?

Sure, go on, I say. What's five minutes between friends.

My Sullivan boy sneaks away on me neatly. I look up from bagging pork medallions as the doorbell rings his theft from my shop. I watch the wind play with him as he crosses the street. He peers through the gate to my aunt's abandoned yard, where he keeps a few sheep. I imagine bleating as he slots through.

Poor old Mrs. Sullivan was a lovely woman, says Susie's mother. That fella's big into the horses, you know. At least his father only bet on them.

That was my grand-aunt's bakery, I say. It's still strange to stand here, looking at it from across the street.

Susie's mother brightens up.

Tell me again what your husband's called, she says.

Ludo.

Isn't that gas, like the game.

He's the image of it, I say, but she looks confused.

And he's an Italian?

An Italian stallion, I want to say, horses on my brain, and sex.

Ludo Pellegrini, I say.

Oh, that's lovely. It must be tough being away from him.

I'm at ease in her sympathy, so I don't tell her she's wrong. It doesn't hurt to be untethered. Instead, it's slightly dizzying. There's no one to negotiate my inner life with, and I'm more visible, no family to deflect scrutiny from myself.

I'm doing fine, I say.

You are. Well, I'm away. Call over to me any evening, apart from Tuesdays.

She has already told me she has St. Vincent de Paul on Tuesdays. She said it like the saint himself was coming over. Her words mix with the bell on her way out, and I raise a hand in farewell. All exits are awkward in the empty hours. People prefer if someone else comes into the shop and they can slip out while I serve their replacement. It might be the bell that scares them, making a big deal of their flight. I could adjust it so it only rings on entry. I'd have to rig it up to the outside door handle. I imagine my customers piled up in an electrocuted heap outside the door. The smell I imagine is barbecue.

I draw the scraper over the remainder of the lamb chops; this side, slap, that side.

Never say *nag*. I don't know how to deal with men when they exhale through their noses. I've never expressed my disappointment in someone who's right in front of me. What was it in male upbringing that told them it was all-right to judge openly, whereas my bones learned that it was rude? I judge them inwardly, of course.

Nag. My animal jokes always fall flat. I decide to let meat be meat and stop trying to bring it back from the dead. Meat-is-animal jokes must be done with a kind of glee that I can never sufficiently conjure up. They know I'm faking.

No one has realised I'm a vegetarian, and I'm not really one anymore. I only eat scraps and offcuts because I can't bring myself to throw them away. If I had a dog, I'd be full vegan, maybe. I might be getting a taste for blood. Poor Ludo. He'll never come.

Since I have time, I give serious thought to where Patrick and I would live if we got together, if we were to keep the farm and the shop, the horses, potatoes, abattoir. It's easier to come downstairs to work instead of driving in from the countryside, and I wouldn't find anyone to rent upstairs. It doesn't have its own entrance, and I need the kitchen for breaks during the day. It would be a waste and an inconvenience not to live here, but his house on the farm is lovely. Rolling fields. Quiet. Slurry. A farmer has to rise early, but he isn't exactly milking cows.

What is it about tweed and drink, the smell of cigarettes, a loud voice? A certain type of man has all of that. It's attractive, but I can't tell why. It is, perhaps, a dangerous relinquishing of control; something to do with sex; nothing good to do with a relationship. An inbuilt female charge of self-sabotage placed some time in history when the species survived by force, the violence asserted then still felt now.

He can't be more than twenty-five.

I bring the cleaver, scraper and cutting board to the sink and set the water gushing. I love the word *cleaver*. My favourite used to be *beyond*. When you're beyond something, something big like youth and innocence, the word for where you are is no longer fascinating.

I'm transforming back to a single-thinking entity. I've been in this state of mind as a young woman, but this is different. I'm better at controlling what people think of me now, which gives me more scope to define myself, but I can't help thinking of those vulnerable years, nor wondering if some part of me is still prone to damage. I could have gone to a big city to get lost in a warren of streets. This is not the place to find yourself, though I may find someone to be. It's automatic, how I say what I think they'll approve of. I haven't mentioned that I don't go to Mass. I'm not so false as to go, but I feel it's best not to mention it. No one asks. Maybe they got over that while I was away. I'm always guessing. They must think me old-fashioned because, in my efforts to fit in, I'm talking to them right out of the eighties, but other decades have passed here too. They come and buy my meat, my veg, but even Fran Halloran, for all her wanting our children to be friends, even she wouldn't like her daughter to be stuck behind a butcher's counter.

In half an hour, I'll close the shop, and I'll be alone in this house. I'll wander upstairs to imagine the lives of my predecessors. The shop, I feel I've conquered; the bedrooms upstairs and the bathroom are still not entirely mine. They'll take more than one person to fill.

Stuart the dentist orders minced beef, and, after a pause, he adds the explanation, Spaghetti Bolognese. He might be pointing out that he's not making anything special for dinner, or he could be alluding to my Italian connection. For all I know, he might believe there's a special way to mince beef like they do in Bologna.

I observe how the mincer transforms recognisable limbs into marbled strings. It's not the destruction I like, simply the pattern on the bumpy coils. It makes the fat palatable. No one actually eats the strips of fat along the edges of chops and steaks, though the meat would look wrong without them. The fatty edges are only a garnish, something to scrape off a plate into the dog's dish when you're finished. Those small, brown bins for food waste must be full of this pale wobble.

For years, Ludo didn't have to think about his weight, and that was part of his charm, this belief that he could eat what he wanted, behave how he liked. He felt he was entitled to it all and more, and now I think I was attracted to him because he was what I wanted to be. I make my dinner from leftover scraps, but I do favour the lean cuts.

It's cold in here, all this early-summer day. The flesh—I must stop calling it that—the meat is cold by necessity. Low temperature is all it takes to change a thigh to a chop. Nothing is alive that is this chilled.

I clench my fists and stretch my fingers out to stars. I wear loose shoes and do the same to my feet, in turn, all day. I wear woollen long-johns and thick-soled woollen socks meant for hiking. I am a living thing in a place for the dead. The graveyard, sun-dappled or windswept, is nothing to this. The locals come to me for dead things. I provide. I often look over to my veg section. People buy more of the pre-washed and topped roots, but I keep others displayed with their earth still on them and their inedible greenery gushing towards the sun.

Susie Casey asks me about my family again. She's only making conversation. I imagine telling her how little I care, that I value myself most. Is it so bad? I could have waited for my children to leave me, but I got out first. Empathy and care are all very well, but we all look out from behind our own eyes.

Oh, I don't know, Susie, I say. I don't know at all. What else did you say you wanted?

Divination

Stephen Spratt

Wood (木; mù)

Your heart shines like a star beside the sea,
but I would draw you here, beneath the trees,
to an old grove where a young boy once carved
spells deep into bark of oak, cut and charmed
green birch twigs into chains to kiss your wrists,
built a bower where our little birds might nest.
Then I would keep you here for evermore,
far from the voices calling at the shore.

Fire (火; huǒ)

Hands cupped against the wind and the world,
lit from within like the Tiffany lamp wings
of a dragon enfolding the last of its gold;
it dreamt of a silver coin moon, chasing
it again across the sky till morning,
reimagining, perhaps, the long foretold
disasters that would soon be engulfing
him, cupped though he was against wind and world.

Earth (土; tǔ)

I no longer believe human beings
can achieve escape velocity
unlike the silly boy that I was, filling
up with soil through a mouth of shattered teeth,
roots splitting apart fingers and toes, insects
feasting as I fought like a fool towards
the beckoning light, only to be pulled back
down by hands that grip like the talons of birds.

Metal (金; jīn)

Can you see the stars birthing iron at night,
hear the young ones taunt the core beneath
us with tales of the surgical knives
they'll become in some future of steel,
feel the old core shiver as waves of relief
whisper the far worse fate avoided? *Godlike,*
excising multitudes of undreamt dreams
to save, or just assuage, a single life.

Water (水; shuǐ)

Oceans hold the secrets of the universe
in spells of quantum chemistry and curses hurled
against rock. We too encode our secrets
at the sub-atomic scale, then forget
the worst ones as best we can, unaware
that even silent songs sing, like malware.
At the shore, pink blossom falls upon my face,
and there you are, moving with a slow grace.

Two Poems
Grace H. Zhou

Mother Tongue

High tide is coming. Beneath the bridge beneath our feet,
the rush of water. My dad knows how the currents pull,

which spot is good for digging crabs in summer.
The marsh disorients me. Which way is land, is sea?

Crabs like to be in the muddy. I used to flinch
and click-correct his immigrant English.

The *he-she's* casually slipped around,
accent beating down the wrong syllable.

Naming is not always about possession, I realize one night
holding my baby—it is also protection.

When Gang Chen, professor of mechanical engineering at MIT,
was arrested in his kitchen by federal agents for supposed espionage,

he wanted to shout over the brewing coffee to his wife—
anything you say can be used against you—

but he couldn't speak a word, afraid that the familiar
lilt of their mother tongue would mark him as alien.

Alien, from the Latin, "belonging to another."
At its origin, defined not by strangeness, but attachment:

a love note slipped into an envelope and flown to another
city, kingdom, room, where someone cradles your past

like a bruised persimmon. My baby puckers his lips
and the world's sensory-scape comes alive.

We name what we love and in the process
allow ourselves to be renamed.

So I have become one who knows the tired wail
from the hungry. The sour plum from the sweet.

Day by day, we walk the same green patch,
observing what changes, what is constant. I point—

Leaf. Yezi. Listok. Luna. Moon. Yueliang.
In three languages, words bead off my tongue

like the nacre a bivalve makes to shield its soft gut.
One day, something splits open—

Hibernal Lessons

The blackthorns are heavy with fruit this time of year, which
according to the old sayings, is sure sign of a hard winter ahead.

What do I know of hard winters or their auguries.
In the dimming of last September, in a city

where we were passing strangers, ladybugs nudged their way
through our sealed windows before the freeze.

We eased them back out with cupped hands, believing
somehow, this was an act of mercy.

I want you to know there is such a thing as mercy
but I look down and see my fingernails over-

grown and brittle. Somewhere down an alley is a lone
car on ice, wheels in motionless spin.

In my darkest hours, I don't believe in respite,
just the long gun-barrel of time. One thousand years

bracing against parched winds and the ancient
bristlecones of Death Valley are gone, too. Blame a man-

made drought and beetles riding the global supply chain
but I don't want to be needle-leafed, heartwood so tightly wound

just to live for millennia. I want to go from flourish to flourish,
so that even in December, the birds may feast.

A South Ulster Homestead

Mary O'Donnell

On the hill, behind the clustered oaks,
  a home, large enough to rear sturdy kin,
where great aunt Iris also settled
  in a north-facing room with cross-stitch proverbs,
Bible quotations and polished linoleum.

Our square kitchen, yellow-flagged, always scrubbed,
  a blacked range that bellied heat all winter,
the lumbering table where my wife made bread,
  her drift of bran and wheat, buttermilk spatters
sopped clean when round tins slid to oven

and hot air churned its alchemy to raise
  the cross she scored, to split each golden loaf
to quarters. In the dairy, I scalded
  steel milk cans, a mesh of cheese-pans gleaming
amid an airy bite of acid that lingered

from curds and whey. Outside in the garden,
  an old black coach, the disused tram carriage,
follies where our children could dart and play
  during the annual Strawberry Tea,
one war remembered—the first, infernal,

dissolved so many of them, us—by women
  in hats and heels on a dry May lawn.
In time, our numbers shrank. Theirs bloomed.
  They moved in and upwards, claimed some space
in a new desertion, pernicious, Catholic.

In a blaze of ownership, they ripped down
  our centuried lintels, straight-gazing windows,
made them bow, bay, with glittering panes
  when the drumlin sun streamed from the south-west.
They dispensed with milking parlours,

north-facing larders, where pheasants, turkeys
   once hung from string in the run-up to Christmas.
Stacked china pantries absorbed in kitchens
   with granite and chrome, ignored the rites
of use and order, our gardens neat and green

while theirs boomed with borders, swags of colour.
   Like dominos, the decades collapse, erase.
They found their feet, how well they found their feet.
   On the hill, behind the clustered oaks,
their houses, our houses. Their fields, our fields.

Now my ripped ancient hedges—blackthorn, holly—
   make space for tillage, a quick coin.
I turn my face against the sight, see instead
   a fire-breasted robin pipping, pipping,
cheerio-pip-pip for wintering out
   at the back-end of a homestead in time.

Cans
Adrian Martin

1st Prize, Subscriber Flash Fiction Competition

A bag of cans is complete metaphysics.

Listen…

"Cans?"
"Yes"

Then the listless but purposeful walk to the vendor. That's where the God-moment is. You are broke and out of ideas, and yet you still have one idea that will complete you. How can complete defeat also be complete victory?

Cans.

Standards can be raised slightly by applying a bag. That one-molecule-thin plastic membrane charged-for by the retailer is optional. Be comforted that those molecules could not have achieved a finer quantum destiny than to be a part of your event.

Bag of cans.

The walk can be achieved alone, in pairs or in groups. It doesn't matter. A group doesn't turn cans into a party. Nor does being alone turn cans into an inward reflective journey.

Cans has unique economics. You can buy the cheaper variety but not necessarily the cheapest. The best value for money to alcohol content is not obligatory either. You may even be able to afford a luxury brand this time. Or not.

Beer or cider or perry is fine.

You can drink cans without an establishment. Or you can drink cans in bed, or in a hotel room. You can drink cans at a public event, or you can drink cans on your way home from work. You are the licensee.

You are everything and nothing at once.

What can reconcile you to the universe, and the universe to you?

Cans can.

The Trees

Lauren O'Donovan

2nd Prize, Subscriber Flash Fiction Competition

I didn't want to know where dad had done it, the details of it. My uncle said he would tell me if I wanted, but I'd be better off not knowing, not having a clear picture in my mind. But as I drove up the road my father had paved himself across three fields to their new house, I looked at every ancient, gnarled tree, assessing which branches were the right shape, which could have held the weight. I saw my father suspended from each one, waiting, alone in the cold dark, the wind shaking him and pulling at his clothes.

Now it's time to bring my father's body back home, to end where he started in the city of his birth. As the hearse engine starts, the driver tells me gently he had hoped not to see me again so soon, and I reply, gently, that I hope after today we never meet again. It was only six weeks previous we had driven this same route, again three of us in the hearse, but that time it was my step-mother boxed up in cream taffeta and pine, not my father.

We pull around the house, start down the long drive. The driver nods to a solid pair of matching white-washed brick sheds still housing moving boxes and building supplies. 'Best to knock those down, love,' he says, 'Start fresh.' And so, without knowing, he gifts me back the trees.

A Bland Farewell

Radhika Iyer

3rd Prize, Subscriber Flash Fiction Competition

Uncle stood up and grasped the urn filled with Father's ashes. I watched silently as he closed his eyes and chanted some prayers. He removed the cloth covering the mouth of the urn and gently dropped it into the water. The urn hit the water with a small splash. Almost instantly, the grey waters carried it away from the boat. Uncle continued to chant and then lifted a heavy bag filled with some chunky, white stuff and dropped that into the ocean too.

'What's that?', I asked him.

'It's white flour cooked in water. It's just a thick, bland paste.'

'Why are we dropping that into the sea?'

'It signifies tasteless food. It's for the soul. So the soul will see this as earthly matter and will not be drawn back to material life. Then the soul can reject all earthly connections and float towards bliss and nothingness.'

Father loved food and loved eating. Watching him eat was a visual feast in itself. He would mix the right amount of rice with the accompanying dishes and sweep the clump into his mouth, decorated with a sliver of poppadom. At religious functions or weddings, he would provide an uninvited critical review of the food. I imagined Father's soul tearing into the bag of cooked flour paste, scooping a mouthful into his mouth, and launching into a rant of all its shortcomings before giving details on what spices and condiments could turn that bland paste into a tasty delicacy.

1st Prize, Subscriber Poetry Competition

Another Coming

Jamie O'Halloran

Today's Angelus is a thin plonk
like the piano tuner's persistent playing
of one black key. Reminder, it is said,
this midday chime, of the unexpected,
where you might be scraping a carrot
or reading a book and some lambent angel
materialises right there in front of you
with a life-shattering pronouncement,
like the invasion of a sovereign nation
or the shelling of hospitals and sunflowers.

Bethlehem is now.

Stepping Over Bodies on My Way to Work

Eoin Cahill

Turning onto Talbot Street, I pass under the railway bridge
propped up over the road on four fat stilts,
like one of those landing craft used on D-Day.
In its shadow pools of piss and bodies.

"D'ya have a spare fag love?",
asks a body at the door of what used to be a hotel.
        Please pardon our appearance
        as we complete our transformation
says a faded yellow sign in the window.

The past here is a system of fault lines, of fractured plates,
colliding under the surface. Tremors shake the gaunt
buildings, loosening masonry on rooftops
that spits down on the bodies below.

The bodies I step over lie wrapped in wrinkled blankets
of cold concrete. Some try to dig themselves out
but more bricks fall, tucking them in tight.

The past doesn't seem to fall on me in the same way,
just a dusting of debris, on the shoulders of my work coat
that I brush off once inside.

3rd Prize, Subscriber Poetry Competition

In My Dream About the Old House

Lucy Holme

I am in your office emptying the formica pencil-pots with rubber lids—
opening a slim drawer full of copper change. I climb branches of paper-
clips, swim in coagulated ink pool blots. From the window I spy you smoking
by the apple tree. You came back home to take us for a test drive.
I am in a Vauxhall showroom in 1986, the burn of Extra Strong mints
and plastic on new company-car seats. Soon we reach the cliffs, the sea waves
us over and the chilly north-west breeze slaps our ruddy cheeks.
We take seats on the front row bench for Dover's deafening chorus line
while gulls stamp their feet, yell loud enough to wake the worms. Thin,
yellow bills scour gravel for Cornish pasty crumbs.
I am in my bedroom. I remove my infant son from around my neck—
he leaves the imprint of a fresh-sprung tooth upon my cheek. He'd swallow
me if he could. Down stairs we glide, *Hold tight now, see? It's light.*
He takes my hand, calls *falling* with every step as I stroke his sweating brow.
You meet us again in the hallway in a navy suit and wide, striped tie,
in your pocket a pouch of Capstan tobacco flakes. I snatch your spectacles
and put them on to dance and shout *I'm Daddy! Look at me!* The silver smoke
rises. I count the glass brick panes in your eyes, hear the hiss
of the TV coming to life playing the theme to St. Elsewhere. *Sod death*
you say, with a wink. *You'll be all right, love. Have a drink to ease the pain.*
I am in the garage. We cheer with mismatched glasses but I cannot raise
my flute, and bow my head. At the sweet scent of matted grass clippings
from the Flymo, of Dulux paint-splattered rulers bathing in white spirit
I am eight again, playing make-believe. I cannot see the whole picture,
wonder if I ever will. You hadn't smoked for forty years.

Seán Ó Faoláin International Short Story Competition

1st Prize:

€2,000

1-week residency at Anam Cara Writer's & Artist's Retreat

Publication in *Southword 46* (Spring 2024)

Offered a featured reading at the Cork International Short Story Festival
(with four-night hotel stay and full board)

2nd Prize:

€500

Publication in *Southword 46* (Spring 2024)

Four runners-up will be published in *Southword 46* and receive €250 (publication fee)

The competition is open to original, unpublished and unbroadcast short stories in the English language of 3,000 words or fewer. The story can be on any subject, in any style, by a writer of any nationality, living anywhere in the world. Translated work is not in the scope of this competition. There is an entrance fee of €19 per story.

Deadline: 31st July 2023

Guidelines: www.munsterlit.ie

Fool for Poetry International Chapbook Competition

1st Prize: €1,000

2nd Prize: €500

Both receive chapbook publication and 25 complimentary copies

Both offered a featured reading at the Cork International Poetry Festival (with three-night hotel stay and full board)

This competition is open to new, emerging and established poets from any country. At least one of these winners will be the highest scoring manuscript entered by a debutant poet with no previously published solo collection (full-length or chapbook). Up to 25 other entrants will be publicly listed as "highly commended".

Manuscripts must be 16–24 pages in length, in the English language and the sole work of the entrant with no pastiches, translations or "versions." The poems can be in verse or prose.

There is an entrance fee of €25 for each manuscript. Entrants may enter more than one manuscript. The winners will be selected by a panel of renowned poets.

The winning chapbooks will be published by Southword Editions and launched at the Cork International Poetry Festival (2024). They will be for sale internationally through our own website, Amazon and select independent booksellers.

Deadline: 31st August 2023

Guidelines: www.munsterlit.ie

Southword Editor's Poetry Award

€1,000 for the best entry of three poems

One entry only per person

Each entrant for their €20 entry fee will receive a complementary one-year, postage-free subscription to *Southword*

Poems will be read and judged anonymously by Patrick Cotter, current poetry editor of *Southword*

The winning poet will have their three poems published in *Southword*

If you are already a subscriber your subscription will be extended

Once a subscriber, there is the opportunity to enter, for free, other competitions which are for subscribers only

At least twenty other entries will be selected for honourable mention

Deadline: 30th September 2023

Guidelines: www.munsterlit.ie

Contributors

Nathalie Abi-Ezzi is a novelist, short story writer and poet. Her debut poetry collection, *Needle Around her Neck,* was published this year.

Kizziah Burton was recently shortlisted for the Forward Prize for Best Single Poem. This year, she won Third Place in *Mslexia*'s Women's Poetry Competition.

Paddy Bushe writes in Irish and in English. *Peripheral Vision* is his latest collection in English.

Eoin Cahill's poems have recently appeared in *Cork Words 3* and *Black Bough Poetry*. Find him on Twitter @eoinspoems.

Jody Callahan is a fiction writer at work on her first novel. She lives in Northampton, Massachusetts.

Nearing 80, **Simon Peter Eggertsen** came late to poetry after a career in international health. He has degrees in literature, language, law and lives in Montreal.

Blair Ewing is a Baltimore poet. In 2022, he released his 3rd book, *Word of Mouth,* on Apple Music, Spotify, Pandora & other platforms.

Galin Elias Franklin is a lawyer and educator from the United States, currently living in Spain. He studied literature at Harvard University.

Peggie Gallagher's work has appeared in literary journals in Ireland, England and North America. Her first collection, *Tilth,* is published by Arlen House.

Covid's ill wind drove **J.P. Garvey** to submit his stories. He feels especially good to see this one published in *Southword.*

Lucy Holme lives in Cork City. Her debut chapbook *Temporary Stasis* was published in 2022 by Broken Sleep Books.

E.M. Hughes lives and works in the Netherlands. He's winner of the 2022 Seán Ó Faoláin Short Story Competition.

Luisa A. Igloria is a poet and professor in the MFA Creative Writing Program at Old Dominion University, Norfolk VA.

Radhika Iyer writes fiction and creative non-fiction. She has published a collection of short stories entitled *Why Are You Here?*

Karan Kapoor's poems have appeared in *AGNI, Rattle, Poetry Online, North American Review,* and elsewhere. They're an MFA candidate at Virginia Tech.

Anne Kennedy specialises in acrylics and watercolours. Her work is available at Passage West Creates.

Yesol Kim is a student of literature. She lives in New York.

Adrian Martin is a middle-aged fiction writing enthusiast who is slowly working his way into short stories before an obligatory novel.

Aidan Mathews' new collection *Pure Filth* will be published by Lilliput Press in late 2023.

John Minihan was born in Dublin in 1946 and raised in Athy, County Kildare. His photographs have been exhibited throughout the world.

Jenny Mitchell has three collections – two prize winners. *Map of a Plantation* is a required text. *Resurrection of a Black Man* contains three prize-winners. @JennyMitchellGo

Judith H. Montgomery's first collection, *Passion,* received the Oregon Book Award. Her prize-winning narrative medicine chapbook, *Mercy,* appeared in 2019.

Laura Morris is from Caerphilly, South Wales. She is working on a collection of short stories.

Canisio Mudzimu is a Zimbabwean poet and freelance writer who holds an MBA from the University of Zimbabwe.

Lenore Myka is the author of a prize-winning story collection. She's working on a memoir about her adopted home, Florida.

Mary O'Donnell's new poetry *Outsiders, Always,* will be published by Southword Editions in September. Her selected translated short stories will be published in Argentina in October.

Lauren O'Donovan has an MA in Creative Writing from UCC. She won the Cúirt New Writing Prize in Poetry 2023.

Jamie O'Halloran's *Corona Connemara and Half a Crown* is a Fool for Poetry Chapbook. She lives in Connemara.

Abigail Parry's first collection, *Jinx,* dealt in trickery, gameplay, masks and costume. Her second, *I Think We're Alone Now,* is about intimacy.

Gary V. Powell is the author two chapbooks, *Super Blood Wolf Moon* (Kallisto Gaia 2020) and *Permafrost* (Finishing Line 2023).

Greg Rappleye lives in Grand Haven, Michigan. *Barley Child,* his latest poetry collection, is in search of a clever publisher.

Catriona Shine is an Irish-Norwegian writer and architect. Her debut novel will be published by The Lilliput Press in 2024.

Stephen Spratt is a writer and researcher based in Clonakilty, West Cork. His poems have appeared in *Poetry Ireland Review* and elsewhere.

Grace H. Zhou is a poet and anthropologist. She is the author of *Soil Called a Country,* selected for Newfound's 2023 Emerging Poets Chapbook Series.

How to Submit

Southword welcomes unsolicited submissions of original work in fiction and poetry during the following open submission periods:

POETRY

What to submit:	Up to four poems in a single file
When to submit:	1st December, 2023 – 28th February, 2024
Payment:	*Southword* will pay €40 per poem

FICTION

What to submit:	One short story (no longer than 5,000 words)
When to submit:	1st January – 31st March, 2024
Payment:	*Southword* will pay €250 for a short story of up to 5,000 words

Submissions will be accepted through our Submittable portal online.
Visit munsterlit.ie/southword or southword.submittable.com for further guidelines.

Printed in Great Britain
by Amazon

24654566R00061